The Naïve Woman

M.L. Lexi

THE SEQUEL TO THE FEARLESS WOMAN

Titles by M.L. Lexi

The Blind Woman
The Deceitful Woman
The Forgiving Woman
The Grieving Woman
The Guilty Woman
The Loyal Woman
The Noble Woman
The Resolute Woman
The Unfaithful Woman

The Farfalla Family Saga

The Determined Woman
The Persevering Woman
The Invincible Woman

The Fearless Woman Series

The Fearless Woman
The Naïve Woman

Copyright

To my husband, one of the few who understands me

.

Sometimes we don't notice what we see every day.

—M.L. Lexi

.

Prologue

ST. BONIFACE'S AUDITORIUM was packed with proud parents and excited graduates in black gowns waiting for their names to be called to the stage to accept their diplomas. Cell phones held above people's heads recorded videos instantly posted to social media for the world to see.

Cassie Nash's long hair flowed in blonde waves from beneath her cap, and her pretty face was expertly painted for the occasion with muted shades of bronze above the green eyes and pink blush at the cheeks. Her wide, full lips were glossed in ruby-red lipstick.

At twenty-two, Cassie Nash was years older than St. Boniface's graduating class of twenty-seventeen, and her appreciation for the moment surpassed that of her teenage classmates. Taking the diploma Principal Jane handed Cassie, she tightly clamped her hand on the scroll, revelling in her triumph.

A D-student, the decision to drop out of school years earlier wasn't difficult for Cassie to make. Cassie's poor academic marks were part of the reason for quitting high school. Caring for her dying mother, Marilyn Nash, paying the bills, keeping a roof over their heads, and eating ranked higher on the decision-making scale.

Caring for Marilyn demanded all Cassie had in her. Cassie devoted all her time and energy to her mother, and everything else became secondary. Months later, on Marilyn Nash's death, seventeen-year-old Cassie was alone, broke, and homeless. That was when Mrs. Pyre,

Marilyn's boss at the Serenity Nursing Home, and the residents and staff unanimously agreed to take Cassie in. Everyone decided to keep silent about Cassie's moving into a spare room at the retirement home and keep her hidden from the corporate suits. Mrs. Pyre and everyone at the nursing home gave Cassie the support and love a broken, lonely young girl needed.

But all good things must come to an end, and it did for Cassie when corporate questioned why room 822 hadn't generated income for years. Corporate began pressuring Mrs. Pyre and the staff for answers. Mrs. Pyre and everyone at Serenity were family, and Cassie couldn't allow Corporate to threaten their livelihoods and impact the workplace they considered a second home.

Out of options, Cassie left Serenity, the place she considered home, and the people she called family and set off to find Bob Huntley, the man her mother revealed on her deathbed was her biological father.

Bob Huntley wasn't difficult to locate. Bob Huntley was Robert James Huntley Sr.'s only son. Renowned solicitor Robert James Huntley was the man who fought the cigarette companies on behalf of the people whose lives were affected by cancer and other serious ailments and won billions of dollars on their behalf. Robert James Huntley's story was spread on social media and the internet for all to read. Tracking Robert James Huntley's son Bob Huntley was simple for a seventeen-year-old computer-savvy girl.

Cassie's trepidation that Bob Huntley would turn her away was counterproductive. Bob warmly welcomed Cassie and let her into his life when she appeared at his front door. It did not take long for Cassie and Bob to become the family they both lacked. Cassie and Bob enjoyed one another's company and took care of each other.

But all good things must come to an end, and a few months after their reunion, Bob was diagnosed with glioblastoma multiforme, a lethal brain tumour. Cassie once again found herself losing the only family she knew.

But family didn't have to be a blood connection. Family was those who were there for you when you needed them, the people you connected with. For Cassie, it was Olivia Falco, Bob's long-estranged wife.

"So, will you do it, Olivia? Will you raise my daughter as your own? Will you teach her how to be the type of woman you are? I want her to grow up to be as strong as you are. I want her to be the fearless woman you are." That was Bob's request on his deathbed, and Olivia didn't hesitate to say yes.

From the auditorium's stage, Cassie looked out to the audience and saw the people she now called family cheering. With a huge smile, Cassie waved her diploma in the air. Olivia and her partner, Dr. George Papadopoulos, rose to their feet and loudly clapped. Olivia's sister Lottie, her husband Ken, and their daughters, Juliette and Lexi, woohood as loud as they could. Then there were Sondra and Malcolm, friends extraordinaire, who loudly shouted their support.

Those people were Cassie's family now and as loyal a family as she knew.

After years of death and misery, there were no dark clouds in Cassie Nash's life, only sunshine. Cassie was enrolled in the nursing program in the fall, leading to her dream job. Caring for people is what she was good at and what she intended to do with her life.

But all good things must come to an end, and Cassie's newfound happy life would be upended by the aunt she never met, who believed Cassie was an impostor who wheedled her way into Bob's life and his will for the substantial inheritance she wasn't entitled to.

Part I

The Beginning

We construct our own version of the truth.

—M.L. Lexi

Chapter 1

THE SKY WAS summer blue, and brilliant sunshine fell over the land capped in green where deer, foxes, raccoons, and squirrels scampered. Clear water trickled through the brook, a soothing gurgle. Under the warm breeze, blue jays, sparrows, and orioles flitted through the air before landing on tree branches crowned with budding greenness to chirp in song.

Atop of the green stood the Georgian-style home with a red-brick façade, arched entrance with tall pilasters, and large picture windows. Pristine, sprawling gardens in glorious bloom flanked the home. The house was as impressive as the grounds, which included a paddock, a stable with horses, and a swimming pool. Steeped in history, the Huntley Estate was passed to the generations of Huntley sons until recently when Cassie Nash inherited it from her father, Bob Huntley, on his death.

Cassie lived at the estate with her newfound family, Olivia, George, and Oreo, a black and white Maltese Shih Tzu who thought of himself as human. As part of Cassie's pay-it-forward promise, Sondra and Malcolm lived rent-free in the guesthouse, two hundred yards to the left of the main house.

Olivia walked onto the patio and cleared her throat to get Cassie's attention, who looked miles away. "Freshly brewed," Olivia said, offering Cassie the coffee cup.

Olivia wore jeans, a white tapered shirt, and red patent moccasins. Her shoulder-length chestnut hair was clipped with a black claw. She wore no makeup, and her

Mediterranean olive skin, darkened by the summer sun, had a healthy glow.

Eyes the colour of moss looked up from her trance to Olivia. "Thank you." Cassie wrapped her hands around the mug, watching the steam curl and dissipate into the hot morning air. Cassie looked summery in white shorts and a sunflower-yellow tank top. Her blonde hair fell around the youthful, tanned face. Her bare feet were propped on the padded rattan ottoman.

"I thought I'd take a break from writing. Are you interested in the company?" Olivia sat on the adjacent chair when Cassie nodded.

Olivia enjoyed this time of day when Sondra, Malcolm, and George were at work, and all was peaceful, calm, and still. Olivia loved each of those people from the depth of her heart, but sometimes, she needed to check her mind out of the moment to gather her thoughts before sitting down at her desk to write.

Olivia's recently published eBook, The Fearless Woman, was getting less than the anticipated traction, but it was early days. She had scaled many mountains in her lifetime, and slow sales of her first book wouldn't discourage her from fulfilling her writing dream and telling the many stories she had in her.

"You looked to be deep in thought." Olivia mimicked Cassie and stretched her legs, setting her feet on the ottoman.

Cassie quietly stared into the dark liquid in her coffee cup momentarily. "Just thinking about stuff."

"Care to share? I'm a good listener." Olivia's eyes followed a pair of hawks majestically sail across the sky and disappear among the thicket of tall pine trees.

"I was thinking of Daddy. We used to sit here in the afternoons. Him with a glass of Johnny Walker, me with a cup of coffee and a cigarette, and take in the view and talk.

We had a lot to catch up on." Cassie took a sip of her coffee because it was in her hand.

"Yes, I imagined you did." Olivia took a swig of the coffee in her hand.

"During one of those afternoons, he told me about his illness and you. He told me what he did to you and George. How he came between the two of you because of the shallow, petty man he was, talked you into marrying him, and then proceeded to mistreat you all through your marriage." Cassie lifted her gaze to meet Olivia's eyes. "Daddy was very sorry he hurt you."

Olivia nodded with great understanding. "He made his amends. Because of Bob, George and I came together after all these years."

Cassie gave Olivia a pointed look. "You love George very much."

The comment conjured up pleasant thoughts that put a big smile on Olivia's face. "I do. George was my first love. We were good friends in high school before I fell in love with him. In my opinion, that is the best form of relationship evolution. Connecting with George after all these years and resurrecting those feelings and knowing they're as strong as they were in our teens is," Olivia searched for the right word and came up with, "glorious."

Cassie saw the depth of emotion swaying into Olivia's eyes as she spoke and envied her. She hoped to one day feel the love for a man Olivia felt for George. Cassie was young, and there was time to meet her knight in shining armour. Right now, there were more significant concerns crowding her mind.

"But I don't think thoughts of George and me was what filled your thoughts when I came out," Olivia said.

Cassie shook her head. "Thinking about Daddy led me to think of Aunt Michelle."

Olivia's grip on the handle of her cup closed tighter. "What about Michelle?"

"She's the only family I have left, you know?" Cassie glanced sideways at Olivia, then away when she saw her face turn serious.

Olivia hadn't kept her dislike for Michelle Huntley a secret the times Cassie brought her up, and the ireful glint in Olivia's eyes told Cassie today was no exception.

"George, Sondra, Malcolm, Oreo, and I are your family, Cassie. You don't need Michelle in your life to complete you." Olivia jumped in to say when Cassie started to open her mouth to finish her thought.

By the elm tree, Oreo rose on his hind legs and barked at the squirrel clinging to its trunk, staring him in the eye and daring him to follow. Oreo did not follow. It wasn't how he rolled. Instead, Oreo did what he did best, he plopped his butt on the grass and gazed soberly at his nemesis.

Cassie put her coffee cup on the table between her and Olivia's chair. "I know, and I love all of you, but Aunt Michelle is…."

"Not the type of person your father was. At least not the person he was toward the end of his life." Impending death affects the human psyche in extraordinary ways, Olivia thought. "Michelle is,"—a ginormous bitch without a conscience—"a strong woman, made from Huntley stock."

Cassie gave Olivia a curious look. "So am I, and I'm not mean or hard, am I?"

Olivia's hand closed over Cassie's. "Of course, you're not, honey, but your DNA is half your sweet mother's, and you weren't bred from birth to be a Huntley as Michelle was."

"What's that supposed to mean?" Cassie's eyes were calm, but her voice was laced with passion.

"All I'm saying, honey, is that you don't know Michelle as I do. She's not a nice person."

"I know she's my aunt, and her sons, William and Harry, are my cousins." Despite her troubled thoughts,

Cassie's lips curved into a soft smile when Oreo charged onto the patio and straight to her. "Tired of that teasing squirrel, are we?"

Oreo barked, jumped onto Cassie's lap, and settled in for head scratches.

"I don't even exist anymore for him, do I? If you recall, mister, you carry my surname," said Olivia. Oreo yawned at her. "Thank you for that."

"He's just tired." Cassie took Oreo's face in her hands. "He's had a busy morning, haven't you?"

Oreo's tongue lolled out in a canine grin, and Cassie rubbed his ears and gave his fluffy head well-deserved scratches.

"Yes, eating, soaking sun on the patio, and provoking head scratches is exhausting," Olivia said.

Cassie let out a soft smile and fell silent for a few seconds. "I want to meet Aunt Michelle, her husband Jackson, and my cousins William and Harry."

"I see." Olivia remained stone-faced, her eyes focused straight ahead at the roll of green that stretched as far as the eye could see.

Only months ago, Cassie was homeless, and now the magnificent home she lived in and the twenty acres of land before her were hers, along with the fifteen million dollars Bob left her in his will. And Michelle Huntley wanted to take it all from Cassie.

By Michelle's reasoning, Cassie had wheedled her way into Bob's life and talked him into believing she was his daughter. Michelle made it clear in her emails to Olivia that she didn't believe Cassie was a Huntley, let alone Bob's daughter. Her boys were Huntley through and through, and the Huntley Estate and the millions Bob left Cassie belonged to them.

Chapter 2

FROM THE OPEN bathroom door, steam mushroomed in a white cloud into the bedroom. The sweet smell of George's Irish Spring soap scented the air. "I think it's time to tell Cassie about the threatening emails you've received from Michelle over the past few months, Livy." George shut the water off and reached for the towel on the bar. "You've managed to keep Michelle in check, which has greatly impressed me. From the tenor of her emails, the woman sounds like a she-devil."

"She is that and more." Olivia removed the mounds of pillows on the bed.

Outside was a dark background with a bright, round moon. In the beams of moonlight, shadows lurked, and the night sounds filled the stillness.

"As formidable as you've become, you and I know you can't hold her off forever. Sooner or later, Michelle will make good on her threat to strip Cassie of everything Bob willed her." George wrapped the towel around his hips and walked to the vanity. He wiped the steamed mirror with his hand until he saw his reflection.

"I know, and the property and money aren't even the issue. It's not as if she will end up homeless again. I still have my house. We can move back when the lease for the tenants occupying it expires." She transferred the pillows to the bench at the foot of the bed

"And I still have mine," George reminded Olivia.

"I'm mostly concerned about Cassie getting hurt and disappointed by the adults in the room. Not to mention, become jaded by the selfishness of the people you look to as a family."

"We're her family."

"We are, but with Bob's death, Cassie feels disconnected and seems to need a familial connection." Olivia stopped to think how she'd feel if she didn't have her sister Lottie when her mother and father died. Olivia could sympathize with Cassie, but Michelle was not the type of family a lost girl in search of familial bonds needed to turn to. "Cassie's too young for so much heartache. She's naïve and has created this fairy tale notion of Auntie Michelle in her head." Olivia air-quoted the words. "Cassie will be devastated when she finds out the truth about the woman Michelle is and what she wants to do to her." Goddamn entitled Huntley's.

The bedroom was as large as the ground floor of the childhood home Olivia left when Cassie asked her to move in with her at the Huntley Estate. When she and George moved in, Olivia made changes to the bedroom to make it homey and hers. A light tan colour to make the space warm and airy and blend with the brown striped marble stone with the embedded rectangular gas fireplace, the room's focal point, replaced the burgundy walls. The floor was dark maple, and white lace curtains that billowed in the light breeze flowing into the room replaced burgundy damask. The bed was king-size with the most costly memory foam mattress Olivia found—one of the few luxuries she treated herself to with the millions Bob left her.

"The truth often hurts, but Cassie needs to know the woman she's determined to call aunt is committed to stripping her of her inheritance and hurting her as much as possible." George picked up the razor to trim the day's stubble.

Olivia stopped folding the bedcover to the foot of the bed and bit the inside of her cheek while she rolled the idea of telling Cassie all through her head.

Michelle's emails to Olivia had become more threatening in the past few months. Olivia fought back and managed to stave off Michelle, but as George said, the lawsuit was an inevitable reality that would come sooner than later. Cassie had to be told.

But Cassie had only now found happiness, and Olivia wanted her to enjoy the moment for as long as she could. Telling Cassie her aunt planned to contest the will to seize everything she inherited from Bob wasn't the type of news a young girl who had recently buried her father and, not long before her mother, needed.

"Of course you're right, but...."

"No buts, Livy. It's time Cassie's told what you know. Especially as she's intent on getting to know Michelle, Cassie needs to know what she's up against." George splashed a light layer of aftershave on his face. "Better to know the truth now, from you, than have her find out through serendipity."

"I'll think about it."

Understanding that was code for "we've exhausted the topic," George closed the conversation with a perfunctory, "You do that."

Olivia knew George was right, but she knew he wouldn't push her. The woman was as stubborn as a mule when she set her mind, and no amount of urging would move her. Then, a strong backbone was one of the traits George loved about the new Olivia.

"Are you coming out here any time soon? I have a bottle of champagne on ice that needs popping." Olivia dabbed *Signorina* perfume on the back of her earlobes, neck, and wrists. She smoothed the white lace babydoll, a gift from Sondra because Olivia was a prude, and a man needed eye candy to rev his motor.

Olivia twisted and turned in front of the dresser mirror. Olivia liked what she saw. She had lost ten of the thirty excess pounds she'd put on over the years. At fifty-five, losing weight was more challenging than she remembered. There were light smile lines at the corners of her mouth and gentle crow's feet at her eyes, and she touched her face with concealer and pink lip-gloss. Her hair was a shiny chestnut, thanks to a very talented hairdresser.

"I'm coming." George slid on the pink boxers with the words HOT FOR YOU in bold black letters on the front—a birthday gift from Sondra.

George looked at himself in the vanity mirror with a slow, curving lip. Only Sondra dared to give a man such an outlandish undergarment, but George had to admit they had come in handy to convey his thoughts when the mood struck.

George stepped out of the bathroom wearing nothing but the boxers. Crossing his arms, he leaned a shoulder against the doorframe. "You hot for me?"

His pale body could use the sun, but as Mount Sinai Hospital's Chief of Neurology, George's schedule didn't permit the leisure time to sunbathe. His short dark hair was slicked back, still damp from his shower. His freshly trimmed stubble traced a strong jawline. Medium height, George was as fit as a man in his mid-fifties could be. And he was all hers.

Olivia snorted a laugh. "Always," she said, walking toward him. She smelled gently of her perfume and looked like a hot virgin in the short, lacy nightgown. And she made the room brighter, George thought. "Are you hot for me?"

"I am so hot for you." George gave her a mischievous smile that made her smile, and when she did, his heart did a quick gallop.

In a low, breathy voice, Heart's Alone flowed from the iPad. The only light in the room came from the Tiffany lamps on the night tables on either side of the bed and beams from the bold and big moon glowing outside the window.

Olivia pulled back from the embrace and looked George in the eyes. "I'll talk to Cassie when the time is right. I promise."

George levelled his dark eyes on Olivia's sea-blue eyes. "I know Cassie is like a daughter to you. She is to me as well. Whatever you decide, I'm here for you. If you want to take Michelle down, I'll support you on that, too ."

"I know you will, but I must do this my way."

"I know you do. All I'm saying…."

Olivia brushed her lips to George's to silence him. "You know how you only told me about your institutionalized wife and that you're still married and would have to remain so out of guilt for her condition only when you were ready? I need to do this when I'm ready."

George's brow winged. "Fine." Resistance was futile, and he was hot for her. "You know I love you, Livy,"

"I do, and ditto. Let's stop talking about Michelle and pop that champagne open."

"Let's leave the champagne on ice and move on to more interesting things," George said, his eyes shining with eagerness.

"Why, Dr. Papadopoulos, without as much as a physical, you made a perfect assessment of my condition," Olivia said, reaching for his hand and leading him to the bed.

Chapter 3

THE OFFICES OF Huntley & Associates, located at the heart of downtown Toronto, filled two floors of a seventy-two-story building on Bay Street with the top solicitors in the country. Olivia walked across the shiny white floor to the elevator bay. She waited with well-dressed men and women immersed in conversation on their cell phones for the elevator to descend thirty floors.

Staring at her reflection on the mirrored wall, Olivia smoothed her long hair and the front of her white sundress. She disputed her simplistic appearance. She should have worn a power suit to portray strength and confidence, not her flowing, sleeveless dress. Olivia debated her hair choice. She should have tied it into a sophisticated twist. The intimidation crept up hard on Olivia at the idea of meeting Michelle. Michelle sucked up all the air from the room and Olivia's confidence—always had, always would.

Stepping onto the elevator, Olivia rode it to the twentieth floor. Fifteen seconds later, the doors opened to a marble entrance, black leather sofas, and a concave receptionist desk. Olivia walked off the elevator with two women and a man who continued their cell phone conversations as they approached the receptionist's desk ahead of her.

The Huntley Knut & Associates sign proudly displayed on the white marble tiled wall in bold black letters caught Olivia's eye. The Knut name was a new addition Olivia didn't expect. Robert James Huntley's plan had come to fruition. Robert's ultimate goal for Jackson Knut to carry his legacy when he disowned his son, Bob, was on display for all to see.

When Robert James Huntley cut Bob out of his life for his many failures that shamed the family and the Huntley name, he moved to mould Jackson into the son he wanted and carry his legacy. Robert offered Jackson a partnership in the firm in return for marrying Michelle and producing the grandsons he wanted. Robert completed his master plan by persuading Michelle to marry Jackson.

Not long after marrying Jackson, Michelle produced two boys and the heirs Robert James Huntley wanted. Michelle chose the names Tommy and Kevin for her sons. Robert, however, deemed the names too pedestrian for grandsons of his. Keeping up appearances trumped all else for Robert James Huntley. William and Harry were the chosen names that ultimately appeared on the boy's birth certificate because of their imperial sound.

As hard as Bob made Olivia's life during their marriage, she often thought Michelle had it worse. When it became clear Bob would not carry on the Huntley legacy, the responsibility rested on Michelle's shoulders. Michelle was forced to lead the life of Robert's design and be accountable to him.

"My name is Olivia Falco," she said, checking in at the receptionist's desk. "I have a three o'clock appointment with Michelle Huntley-Knut."

"It's Ms. Michelle Huntley." The receptionist, a dark-haired, middle-aged woman in a pink jacket with black lapels, corrected. "Let me check you in, Ms. Falco," she added and turned her attention to her computer screen, scanning the calendar and efficiently tapping on the keyboard.

The atmosphere buzzed with office energy. Phones rang non-stop, fingers tapped on keyboards, and legalese talk floated from every conversation. Solicitors, clerks, and assistants flitted through the office in a frantic rush. If there was one thing Olivia didn't miss, it was the hustle and bustle of work life.

"You're checked in, Ms. Falco. Please have a seat. Kayla will be out in a few minutes to take you to see Ms. Huntley." Pasting the smile fit for a receptionist on her face, the hazel-eyed woman relayed the instructions and waved Olivia to the waiting area.

Olivia's wait was a short three minutes when Kayla Fletcher, a severe-looking, plump woman in her early sixties with hair as dark as her eyes tied into a neat bun above her head, walked to the reception desk. She wore a navy blue power suit with a brown-coloured blouse beneath and matching sling-back shoes. After a short conversation with the receptionist to have her point Olivia out, Kayla walked to the sitting area.

"Ms. Falco, Ms. Huntley is ready for you. Please follow me," she said in a mechanized chant. Olivia wondered how many times daily she had to say the words.

Framed prints, possibly originals—Olivia was a plebeian when it came to art—of Italian landscapes hung from steel-gray walls. Amongst the art were plaques acknowledging Michelle's philanthropy to the women's and children's charities she supported. Winding their way through the maze of cubicles, Kayla engaged Olivia in small talk: How was the weather and did she find the trip busy?

"Here we are, Ms. Falco. May I get you something to drink, water or coffee?" Kayla efficiently offered, and when Olivia declined, she invited her to sit at the guest chair facing Michelle, who was on the telephone. "Mr. Knut is in court, Ms. Huntley," Kayla said once Michelle ended the call. "I left a message for him to call you the moment he steps away."

Olivia wasn't sure what impressed her most that Michelle had the gumption to revert to her maiden name from the hyphenated Huntley-Knut rendition she adopted seconds after her marriage vows or that she had her assistant call her husband on her behalf. Modern days.

Michelle looked at her assistant when she returned the telephone handset to its cradle. "Thank you, Kayla," she said, then turned her attention to Olivia, her eyes lingering on her momentarily.

Olivia's enviable olive skin, bronzed darker by the summer sun, looked smooth against the white linen of her sundress. Luxuriously dark and shiny hair spilled around her face, painted in bronze tones. Her tan legs were bare, and she wore Hermès slide sandals at her feet. The matching handbag hung at her elbow. Luxuries Olivia could only afford with her brother's money, Michelle thought.

"You look well, Olivia. A life of leisure agrees with you."

Olivia understood the comment alluded to her inherited money, and her brows raised evenly. Once a bitch, always a bitch. "You also, Michelle."

Much like her mother used to be, Michelle carried herself with grace and understatement. Her long copper-blonde hair floated in shining waves around a face with high cheekbones, large green eyes, and a perfect nose. Michelle's face was expertly made, and Olivia wondered if she had a makeup artist on the payroll.

Michelle wore a camel-colour wrap-front dress with a black belt. A white gold Gucci chain hung from her neck, and diamonds adorned her earlobes, wrist, and finger. She was tall with a lithe body acquired from the daily five-mile runs that began at the high school track and field meets and persisted until today. Perfection was Michelle's middle name.

"Well, now that we have evaluated one another's appearance, let's get to it. I have an actual important meeting to get to in twenty minutes."

"I see that Huntley charm lives on." Olivia sat back in her chair and crossed her legs as a show of confidence. Michelle's Darth Vader force had always intimidated Olivia, but not today.

"I see the Falco sense of humour persists," countered Michelle. "Let's cut to the chase. If you're here to stop me from contesting Bob's will and securing what is rightly mine, you've wasted a trip." Michelle's green eyes held Olivia intently, looking for a sign of vulnerability, and to her surprise, she saw none.

"Why do it, Michelle? You have more money than you need. This firm alone must be worth millions."

Michelle shook her head. "That has no bearing on anything. My brother's mind was questionable in his last months, and I intend to prove it. He willed the money and family home to that woman under duress."

"The woman's name is Cassie, and how would you know the state of Bob's mind toward the end of his life? You didn't call or visit him after I told you he had days to live." Olivia watched Michelle's mouth set in a thin line. "If this is about money, Michelle, assure me you'll leave Cassie alone, and I'll happily turn my share to you."

Michelle arched one thin blonde brow. "She isn't yours and Bob's, is she?"

"No. Bob refused to give me children," Olivia said firmly, refraining from tightly fisting her hands around the chair's arm. "But Cassie is a Huntley, and that money and the property belong to her. She legitimately inherited it. She was there for Bob when you weren't. She cared for him as you never would, your own brother."

"Stop with the histrionics, Olivia." Michelle rested her elbows on the armchair and tented her fingers. "I owed Bob nothing. I was his younger sister, and he was never there for me. Why would you think I owed him anything?"

"He wasn't there for me during our marriage. He did despicable things to me, but I cared for him during his last days of life," Olivia replied in one breath.

Michelle's answer was an icy smile. "Fifteen million dollars is quite an incentive. You'd be surprised what people will do for that sum of money. They might even swallow the last ounce of pride they have left."

Olivia's eyes went hard as stone. "I didn't know about the money, and as I said, I'm willing to turn it over to you."

A slow smile slid across Michelle's face. "Oh, you will eventually. I'm challenging your inheritance also."

Confused eyes stared back at Michelle. "But I just said I would willingly give it to you."

"Where would the fun be in that? Besides, I need to contest your inheritance…."

"To add weight to your ridiculous claim of Cassie's illegitimate inheritance," Olivia finished.

"And I thank you for volunteering to hand the money over. It makes my argument that you and she coerced Bob in his weak state to will the money to both of you that much easier to prove." Michelle reached for the telephone when it rang. "Yes, Kayla, I'm done here." Michelle listened for a moment. "Yes, put Jackson through. Hi, honey," Michelle spoke with a sweetness Olivia didn't believe she possessed. "I wanted to remind you about our dinner tonight with the boys. Harry and William called to confirm they'll be home at seven."

Olivia watched the rush of emotions cross Michelle's face as she listened to Jackson. Everything about Michelle changed, and the confidence and hardness she exuded moments ago dissipated like smoke in the wind. Michelle's thin shoulders hunched, her eyes filled with hurt and distress.

"But the boys are bringing their girlfriends to meet us," Michelle's defeated tone took Olivia by surprise.

Olivia saw in Michelle's eye what she had felt the entire time she was married to Bob: betrayal, defeat, and a tremendous amount of disappointment and pain. That was the look of an unloved woman whose husband's indiscretions were too many to bear.

Forgetting herself or Olivia's presence, Michelle slammed the receiver in its cradle.

"What are you looking at?" Michelle's voice was raw with anger.

"I'm sorry, Michelle." There was a glimmer of understanding in Olivia's eyes, of knowing what Michelle was going through. "I should get going."

Nothing broke an aggrieved woman worse than the pitiful look from another woman, especially if that woman was Olivia. "Well, you said you were leaving," Michelle snapped, propelling from her chair, walking to the sideboard, and pouring herself a drink. "And, Olivia, don't forget, I'm coming hard for you and that tart impersonating to be Bob's daughter. Best prepare for a hard fight because I'm coming for both of you." Michelle tossed back the shot of whiskey.

"She's not a tart, Michelle and like it or not, Cassie's a Huntley." Olivia's voice was polished and calm.

"Get out." Michelle refilled her glass and tossed the second drink back.

At the door, Olivia paused and then turned slowly back. "You took the step to rid yourself of your hyphenated identity. Another step forward, and you'll find what you're looking for. Even you deserve love, Michelle." Olivia said and walked out.

Chapter 4

NOTHING HAD CHANGED. Michelle could still manage to set Olivia on edge. Leaving Michelle's office, with Olivia's stomach muscles clenching into a tightly wound knot of nerves, she headed to the nearest coffee shop for a calming cup of green tea. The tea failed to settle Olivia's nerves, and she followed it with a double shot of strong espresso, a blueberry muffin, and a bagel with cream cheese. Damned be the diet.

When all the food only made Olivia feel sick, she dragged herself to her car to head home.

Oliva hadn't expected to sway Michelle's mind from going through with her plans to hurt Cassie, but she had to try—for Cassie. Michelle was tenacious when she set her mind and was as determined now as she was one year ago to go through with her plan to strip Cassie of her inheritance. Worse, Michelle wanted to out Cassie as a non-Huntley. That would break Cassie, who, after losing Bob, needed a family and belonging.

Now, at the end of her rope, Olivia decided it was time to tell Cassie all.

Turning onto the northbound ramp to Highway 404, Olivia composed the speech in her head. No matter how Olivia spun the words, the outcome was the same. Olivia flipped the radio to a jazz station. The brassy, smooth sounds would help her think. It didn't.

Forty minutes later, pulling into the driveway of Huntley Estate, Olivia didn't have the flowery words she hoped to convey the bad news to Cassie. Olivia decided brutal honesty was the only way to do it.

Olivia found Cassie at the pool swimming laps with Oreo by its edge, keeping up with her and barking excitedly. The early evening sun was beginning to slip away, painting the sky in shades of yellow and orange. The air was redolent with the smells of summer heat, the pool's chlorinated water, and mowed grass.

"Come sit with me, Oreo." Olivia sat on a lounge chair poolside, and Oreo raced forward with his tongue lolling and jumped to settle beside her. "You're having a ball here, aren't you, boy?" Oreo put his head on Olivia's thigh and looked at her. "Well, get your fill, Oreo, because we may not be here long."

Oreo covered his face with his paws as if understanding Olivia's words.

Cassie swam to the lip of the pool. "You should come in for a swim. The water's nice and warm at this time of day." Her neon pink bikini glimmered under the rippling water.

"It does look inviting, but not right now. I want to talk to you." Olivia reached for the towel on the lounge chair and held it up to Cassie when she pushed herself out of the water.

"Is everything okay, Olivia?" Cassie patted herself dry and slipped into her shorts and polo shirt. The outline of her bikini came through as the dampness transferred to her top and shorts.

"Let's take a walk," Olivia said, and with a big grin, Oreo jumped off her lap and did his tippy-tap dance.

"He wants to." The worry in Olivia's eyes made Cassie's brow furrow. "Are you sure everything's okay, Olivia?"

"Walk with me, honey." Olivia with Cassie, in silence, walked through the estate's grounds while Oreo disappeared in and out of the brush, tending to his needs and barking at anything that moved.

Olivia's instincts told her it was best not to say much, that perhaps Cassie had to arrive at those truths herself to see Michelle for who she was. But Olivia's meeting with Michelle dictated otherwise to save Cassie the heartache. Cassie had to know the disappointment she would feel if she pursued a relationship with Michelle.

Oreo walked out of the brush. His eyes were aimed at the Monarch butterfly that landed on his nose and chose to remain there. Cassie giggled a young, girlish laugh, and Olivia thought how good it was to see her smile.

Cassie had endured too much pain and disappointment in her short life. Caring for a dying mother and becoming homeless could take a toll on anyone, let alone a girl in her late teens. When Cassie found the father, who, until recently, was a mystery, Bob was diagnosed with a lethal brain tumour. Once again, Cassie had to care for the parent who wouldn't be in her life for long. Now, in search of her last familial link, Cassie was setting herself up for more letdown.

"Let's sit here." Olivia pointed to the fallen tree by the brook.

Water chugged over rocks in the stream that wound through the estate to join the main artery on the south end. The woody aroma of soil hung in the air. Oreo lapped water from the stream and then ran in and out, barking when the bullfrog, who lazed on the rock as the water streamed past, croaked.

"You look tense, Olivia. What's wrong? Tell me." Cassie's face glowed from being out in the sun all day while reading the Florence Nightingale book Olivia gave her.

"I went to see Michelle at her downtown office this afternoon."

That got Cassie's attention. "Oh. What about?"

"To talk…." Olivia hesitated. There were no good words to say what she had to tell Cassie, and she point-blank said, "I've been getting emails from Michelle since the day following the reading of Bob's will."

Cassie's brow furrowed, and confusion filled her eyes. "I don't understand."

"Michelle's not happy with Bob's assets and money distribution and has threatened to contest the will. She believes the money was ah … wrongly distributed."

"Does that mean she wants some of it?"

Oreo lost interest in the croaking frog and moved on to chasing his nemesis when he spotted the squirrel by the Linden tree staring at him.

"She wants it all. She claims you, and I don't deserve it. Michelle believes we manipulated Bob by taking advantage of his frail state of mind to give us the money." Olivia's eyes remained focused on Cassie's face for her reaction.

Cassie shrugged her shoulders. "I'll give it to her if she doesn't believe I rightly inherited it."

Olivia's lips stretched out in a soft smile. That was the response she expected from Cassie. "She wants the Huntley Estate too. The home and the land."

Cassie gnawed on the side of her cheek now as her stomach churned. A cigarette would be the perfect calming tool, then. If only Olivia hadn't forced her to give the habit up when she moved into her home.

"I've been homeless and made a new home for myself, and I know how to do without if I have to do it again," Cassie said in a low voice.

Olivia wrapped an arm around Cassie. "Honey, as long as I'm alive, as long as George, Sondra, and even Malcolm, God help me, are on this earth, you will never be homeless again. We won't allow it."

The milk of human kindness, Cassie thought, and a smile played across her face. "Thank you, but I think I may be the one looking after Malcolm." Cassie's comment elicited a knowing look from Olivia.

"You're not wrong there. My house is rented, and once the lease expires, we could move back. It's not as grand as this place, but it is home. We also have the option of George's home, which is bigger, and he hasn't sold it yet. I'm saying we have options, and you will never be homeless."

Oreo barked and chased the squirrel around the tree. Once he lost interest, he walked to where the women sat, spread out on the grass before them, and yawned.

"I liked it at your place, and Oreo did too. Didn't you, boy?" Oreo barked before he raised his paw to scratch himself behind the ear. After a moment, Cassie said, "Maybe if I talk to Aunt Michelle, she'll change her mind."

"I don't think she will, honey. She's adamant about taking everything from us. She has filed a notice of objection, which she had her assistant present to me on my way out of her office." Olivia reached into her dress pocket and handed the envelope to Cassie. "She's looking at stripping us of everything down to the kitchen sink."

Cassie's mouth hung open as the situation became more of a reality than an abstract concept. "Why does she want to do this? Aside from not needing the money, she's my aunt. What if I talk to her? What if I tell her Daddy said he wanted me to live in the home he grew up in? Maybe she'll change her mind then."

"She won't, honey." Olivia brushed strands of Cassie's wet hair from her face. "And she'll hurt you if you give her a chance. It's what Michelle does."

Cassie pushed to her feet, startling Oreo out of his slumber. "You don't know that, and I told you I can take care of myself. I want to talk to her myself." Cassie's firm tone told Olivia there was no changing her mind.

Olivia flicked her eyes to the sky. "All right. Just remember that Michelle is a solicitor, conflict is her specialty, and antagonizing is what she does for a living."

Cassie dismissed the comment with a wave of her hand. "She won't do that to me once she meets me. I'm her family." Seeing the worried look on Olivia's face, Cassie said, "I told you I can take care of myself, Olivia."

Olivia gave Cassie a half nod, thinking some lines couldn't be uncrossed.

Chapter 5

"TOMORROW MORNING, I'M calling Auntie Michelle's office to schedule a meeting with her. What do you think about this outfit to meet with her? Does it say professional and business-like yet look familyish?" Cassie asked Oreo, holding the suit against her as she stared at herself in the mirror.

Hearing his name, Oreo, comfortably spread out on Cassie's bed, raised his head. Lifting one eye and then the other, he stared at Cassie.

"Yeah, you're right." Cassie shook her head, and with a dismissive shrug, she changed into a red thigh-high jacket over a white blouse and white slim ankle-high pants. Studying herself in the mirror, Cassie stood on her toes to give herself height. "I need pumps. I'll borrow Olivia's white four-inch Gucci pumps and matching handbag. That'll complete the elegant and sophisticated business look I aim for."

Oreo barked his tacit agreement.

Cassie fell onto the edge of the bed covered in pink, making Oreo bounce a few inches off the mattress. She lay down on the bed and stared at the ceiling, a thoughtful expression sliding on her face. "I wonder if Auntie Michelle is as mean as Olivia says she is. You know, sometimes women are very nasty toward each other."

Cassie had the pot lights on the flat bedroom ceiling on a low dim and the lamps on the night tables on. From the speakers, Adele graciously wished the man who left her the best. The bedroom was a mirror reflection of Olivia's, with walls painted in vibrant lemon-yellow. The room smelled of the lavender fragrance flowing from the burning candles on the dresser. The floors were dark wood, as was the king-size bed. The tall windows on opposite sides of the bed delivered a view of the night sky and the moon shining against the velvet-black backdrop.

"Daddy told me Aunt Michelle was a force to be reckoned with, but neither got along with the other. Daddy didn't know his sister and didn't try to get to know her." Cassie stroked Oreo's fur as he slid into sleep. "Imagine that. As an only child, I always wished for a brother or sister, and they had the benefit of each other and could barely stand one another."

Oreo's snores eclipsed the liquid strains of Ed Sheeran, reminiscing about love. Cassie cranked the volume up.

"Truth is, I don't think Daddy got along with many people, but that's because people didn't understand him." Cassie rolled to her left and draped an arm over Oreo.

"I still don't understand why Daddy hurt Olivia as he did. He never told me why he married her. I suspect it had something to do with George because he wanted to help him reconnect with Olivia at the end of his life. I'm glad Daddy did. Better late than never, I guess. No two people were made for one another, as George and Olivia. Even knowing they can't marry anytime soon because of his wife, they're happy together. Olivia deserves all the love George has in him for her. She's a good person." Cassie curled against Oreo and mulled that in her head. "Who else would promise Daddy to care for the daughter he barely knew? For all Daddy knew, I wasn't his daughter."

There were times Cassie wondered that herself. She and Bob differed in so many ways. Bob liked onions, and Cassie detested them. He was judgmental with a hot temper. Cassie was the opposite of that. Bob had hazel eyes, and hers were green. Her hair was blonde, and his hair was dark.

Her birth certificate said Bob Huntly was the father, but now, Cassie had doubts and needed to quell them. If Bob weren't her father, the truth would come out. Secrets always do.

"I know that Olivia warning me about Auntie Michelle is her way of protecting me, and I'm grateful," Cassie said to Oreo. "But with Mom and Daddy gone, I need to connect with my bloodline. Auntie Michelle and William and Harry are blood relatives." Cassie let out a long yawn. "Meeting with Auntie Michelle will make her realize I'm real and that aside from William and Harry, I'm a part of her bloodline. I mean, she can't dismiss that." With the pleasant thought rolling in her head, Cassie fell asleep.

Chapter 6

OLIVIA SHUT DOWN her laptop when she heard the patio door slide open, and George walked out into the night's heat with glasses and a bottle of wine. He'd showered the day off and slipped into a white T-shirt, pleated chinos, and tan loafers. He looked and smelled clean and fresh.

"It's tranquil without Oreo roaming around and barking at the sounds of the night." George handed Olivia the wine glass.

"He's with Cassie in her room. I've been disowned." Olivia had changed from the white sundress into purple cropped pants and a matching tank top. She traded high-heeled sandals for comfortable ballerina shoes. "Best friend, my foot."

"He knows you traded down to me as your companion. I promise to be more loyal and stick it out with you." George's knee bumped companionably against Olivia's.

"I'm holding you to that, Dr. Papa." Olivia leaned closer and kissed George on the mouth, tasting the Merlot on his lips.

A full moon on the horizon floated its gentle glow over the landscape below, casting mysterious shapes and shadows. The howl of foxes was heard as they moved through the land, searching for their meal. Chirping crickets, the high-pitched buzzing of cicadas and the occasional croak of frogs created a symphony of peaceful sounds and an enchanting atmosphere.

"How's your next book coming along?" With half a glass of wine in, George had shaken the stress of his long day at the hospital and looked relaxed. "Isn't that what you were doing on your laptop?" George said when she gave him a puzzled look.

"Yes, that's exactly what I was doing. My next book is coming along great." Olivia turned her embarrassed eyes away from George and stared at the wine in her glass. "Just fine. This quiet inspires my writing juices."

"Never play professional poker, Livy. You're a terrible liar. You weren't writing. You were checking on your book sales. Am I right?"

Olivia swallowed and looked away. "Three hundred dollars of sales after months. I'm dying here."

George stifled the grin that wouldn't be conducive to what he planned for them later and was careful with his voice, easing it out in a steady tone. "Stop torturing yourself by checking your sales daily and let it happen. It's a great book, Livy. It needs traction, and that's not easy for a new author."

Her lower lip pushed out slightly. "You say that because it's my book, and as my loyal companion and someone hoping to get lucky tonight, you must say nice things."

The floodlights beneath the pool's water shot bright light, making the water look bold and blue. The smell of chlorine was strong in the air.

A smile flickered in George's eyes. "Am I that obvious?"

Olivia's brow winged. "Never play professional poker."

Now, his brow shot up. "Touché, but when have you known me to praise when not deserved? I'm a doctor who routinely delivers terrible news to patients. Telling the truth, good or bad, is what I do." George stretched his legs and crossed his feet at the ankles. "Your book has been available for sale for only a few months. Some of the best authors waited years to get significant sales. You're a new author and must be patient, grasshopper."

Olivia bit down on the corner of her lip. "Patience is not a strong suit of mine."

"This I know." George spotted two pairs of glaring eyes scurrying in the brush in the dark distance. Raccoons, he surmised. If they weren't vigilant, the foxes would be feasting on raccoon meat tonight. George wondered what that experience was like.

"I went to see Michelle this afternoon," Olivia said after the shared silence.

"Oh. You didn't mention you were meeting with Michelle today."

"I didn't because I hadn't planned it. I had a momentary lapse of judgment this morning and called Michelle. As luck would have it, when I called her office to schedule the meeting with her assistant, Michele spoke to me directly and pencilled me in her calendar for this afternoon." Olivia sipped at her wine to wash the bad taste the memory brought up.

"I thought you told me she's one of the top solicitors in the city."

"She is." Olivia took a small swallow of her wine.

"So, how did you get an appointment to see her so quickly? You'd think her schedule would be booked weeks in advance."

"Luck was on my side." Olivia's voice was laced with sarcasm.

Sounding as if Olivia needed an infusion of alcohol, George picked up the bottle of wine and refreshed her glass and his. "I gather the meeting went as badly as expected."

Olivia's agitation surged, and she rose to pace the patio. "Worse." She took a deep swallow from her glass.

"Tell me everything," he said because telling Olivia that was the outcome to be expected or hitting her with the proverbial I told you so was futile when her temper flared hot.

Olivia told him about their conversation. The more she told George, the tighter her muscles bunched up on her neck and shoulders. "She's going through with challenging the will. Her assistant served me the papers on my way out of her office, and I stupidly accepted them after months of dodging. The papers say she's bringing a motion to prove the will is in solemn form. Failing that, she will sue us for everything Bob left us. There's a lot of legal gobbledygook in the papers I don't understand. Christ! Solicitors are a special breed, aren't they?"

"Many of my colleagues agree with you." George watched her pace back and forth, drinking wine as her mind raced.

"I shouldn't have gone to see Michelle." Olivia heaved a sigh of deep regret. "I've managed to deflect her nasty emails for the longest time, but no, I had to see her."

"You did it for Cassie." George pointed out.

"How did that work out for me?" Olivia said hollowly. "First thing tomorrow, I'm contacting a solicitor." The dull ache at the base of her temples intensified at the idea of what she was in for going up against Michelle.

"I have the name of a great solicitor who owes me a favour for saving his life. I'll call him tomorrow and put him in touch with you."

"Great. Great." Nerves bouncing, hand flailing in the air, Olivia recounted every detail of her meeting with Michelle between sips of wine. "She says Cassie and I took advantage of Bob's fragility and manipulated him into giving us the money and property. I volunteered to turn over my money, but she refused. You know what she said?"

George thought he saw her nose flare like a bull's bracing to charge. "I can't imagine."

"'Where would the fun be in simply accepting it?'" Olivia mimicked Michelle's voice.

Unlike Olivia, George took his time with the wine, sipping it slowly and letting it sit in his mouth before swallowing it. "If a fight is what Michelle wants, a fight is what she'll get. We'll fight back as hard and dirty as she does. Fight fire with fire, I say."

Olivia stopped pacing and turned to George. "I'm just venting. I don't mean to drag you into this. You're busy and stressed enough with work."

"If this is important to you, it's important to me." George's voice was so mild in contrast to hers. "We're kicking that bitch's ass, and you and Cassie will keep every dime Bob intended you to have. You forget I was his neurologist and friend at the end of his life. He confided a lot to me. I'm ready and happy to testify on your behalf."

Olivia gave George a serious and focused look and read the sincerity in his eyes. One of the many reasons she loved this man as she did. "I'm all for that, except there's one problem."

"And that would be?" George asked.

"Cassie is intent on talking to Michelle. She thinks she can bond with her and change her mind. Cassie has diluted herself into believing she can make Michelle see reason."

George's surprised eyes held Olivia's. "You told Cassie?"

"Everything. Okay, maybe only as much as she needs to know for now," Olivia added when he cocked a dubious brow. "She can only take so much hurt in one conversation."

George stood and walked to her. "Livy, you can only protect children to a point. You need to ride this out her way." George pressed a finger to her lips to silence her. "Yes, she'll get hurt, but it's what needs to happen, Livy. She's as dogged as you are, and nothing you or I say will change her mind."

"I guess you're right."

"Let Cassie do what she has to and be there for her when she needs you." George extended his hand, and Olivia reached for it. "You need to cool down."

"Where are we going?"

"You think Cassie and Oreo are sleeping?"

"Yes, I believe so."

"Then, we're going skinny dipping in the pool."

"We can't. I can't. There are too many lights."

"The better to see you with, my dear. I like looking at you," George commented with a wink.

George's ravenous look made Olivia forget she had the body of a middle-aged, overweight woman. He made her feel complete and feminine, and after the briefest of hesitations, she let him lead her down the stairs to the pool.

Chapter 7

FOR THE UMPTEENTH time, Kayla hung up the telephone on Cassie. Kayla underestimated Cassie if she thought she would give up on getting slotted into Michelle's busy calendar. Cassie hadn't gotten through life by being a quitter. Besides, she was made of Huntley stock. One way or another, Cassie would see Michelle and have the conversation she must have with her. Cassie would meet the aunt she wanted in her life.

On her way from the family room to the kitchen, Cassie walked past the office. The clatter of Olivia's fingers on the keyboard, followed by a swearing rant, flowed through the closed door. Cassie shushed Oreo when he started to bark for Olivia.

Busy meeting with George's solicitor friend, Joel Rosenberg, Olivia's mind was crowded with thoughts of Michelle, and her creative juices had all but evaporated. Today, though, for the first time in days, Olivia was back to her desk writing and had been hard at work since early morning. Disturbing Olivia when she was on a ranting roll wasn't a good idea.

"Let's go outside, Oreo," Cassie whispered, and Oreo's ears perked up. "You need to take care of business. While you do that, I'll read up on Auntie Michelle. You know, to prepare for my meeting with her. Daddy told me little about her, and none was good. I believe there's good in everyone, and I need to find Auntie Michelle's good side. Everyone has one, right?" Cassie murmured to herself as Oreo followed her to the patio. "I need to know what she's all about."

After a brief stop in the kitchen for a glass of water, Cassie stepped onto the patio. The early morning gray clouds had made way for a bright sun, and the wet blades of grass and leaves on the trees glinted brilliantly under its light. The smell of rich, damp earth lingered in the air, and Cassie filled her lungs.

Sitting at the patio table under the colourful umbrella, Cassie tapped the iPad to life. She typed Michelle Huntley in the search bar. The screen was instantly filled with articles and images of Michelle. Some articles praised her patronage of the women's and children's charities she supported. In many articles, Michelle was lauded as one of a handful of top female solicitors in the country and the fact that she ran a successful firm ranked her achievements all that more impressive.

Michelle had recently won a landmark case against the biggest opioid manufacturer, and the media attention she got was extensive. The two-billion-dollar win to help families affected by the profiteering company that put profit over the welfare of its users got Michelle a lot of press.

Michelle's older history indicated she went by Michelle Huntley-Knut until a few years ago, when she dropped the hyphenation and reverted to her maiden name. Bold move, Cassie thought, rolling the Knut name through her head when it triggered something in her. The name sounded familiar, but Cassie couldn't place it. Cassie dug a little deeper into her memory but came up blank.

Cassie watched Oreo chase his nemesis across the lawn and scurry up the maple tree. For a moment, Oreo stared at the squirrel who munched on the peanut he'd snatched from the feeder Cassie put out.

"Make friends with Nibbles, Oreo. That squirrel will outsmart and outrun you every time, and if you can't beat them, you must join them," Cassie called out.

Cassie wore shorts, a polo shirt, and Roman sandals. Her blonde hair was bound into a ponytail with a blue scrunchie. She wore no makeup, but her summer-bronzed, healthy-looking skin needed no enhancement.

"Silly boy," Cassie murmured when Oreo gave chase to the squirrel, who bounded off the tree trunk and ran across the wet grass.

Back in the kitchen, Cassie poured herself a glass of cold lemonade. She grabbed the salt and vinegar chip bag from the pantry and a milk bone for Oreo. Oreo would need nourishment to replenish his energy when he tired of chasing Nibbles.

Back at the patio table, Cassie set the earbuds in her ears and cranked the volume on her cell phone. Led Zeppelin, an old-school band George turned her onto—and Cassie had to admit were kickass—blared in her ears about climbing the stairway to heaven.-

Cassie clicked on the images tab on her iPad and scanned the many photos of Michelle. There was one of her in a gold sequence gown, her hair bound in a French twist. She radiated an erudite look that came from good breeding.

On either side of the magazine, cover-worthy Michelle stood William and Harry. Looking handsome in tuxedos, ribbed white shirts, and bow ties, William and Harry flashed huge smiles. Tall and statuesque, with blonde hair and blue eyes, the boys were the spitting image of Michelle and Huntley through and through.

Cassie's eyes fixed on the photo when the sense of family struck her hard. Here were her blood relations.

Other photos portrayed Michelle at a children's fundraiser gala, looking tall and elegant with a handful of her staff. Several photographs depicted the Huntley Knut & Associates office. Cassie once again searched her memory for why the Knut name set off the sense of knowing in her. Cassie came up blank until she saw him.

Jackson Knut was two or three inches taller than Michelle was. He had a thick shock of short silver hair with streaks of black through it. Jackson's handsome face was traced in a trimmed, graying stubble. His eyes were ocean blue, and he looked centrefold worthy in the gray, Italian silk suit against a navy shirt and tie. He had a diamond stud in his right ear. Standing beside Michelle, they looked happy, like the successful, beautiful power couple they were.

Cassie focused all of her attention on Jackson.

It took some time, but in the end, Cassie's repressed memory surfaced from the depths of her mind. Cassie sat up with a jerk in her chair when it did.

Enlarging Jackson's picture on her iPad, Cassie studied it more closely. It was him.

Jackson was the man Cassie saw speak to her mother on two separate occasions at the nursing home. What her mother had labelled a discussion looked like a heated argument to Cassie. When Cassie questioned her mother who he was and what he wanted, Marilyn told her Jenson Canute was the son of a resident in her last months of life, and he was having difficulties coming to terms with his mother's impending death.

Jenson Canute was Jackson Knut.

"Christ!" Cassie remained staring hard at the iPad's screen, remembering.

Days after her mother's death, in search of money to cover the funeral expenses, Cassie went through Marilyn's bank account. It was then she uncovered the three thousand dollar monthly deposits made for months by Jenson Canute.

Cassie had so much to deal with after Marilyn's death she forgot about Jenson Canute and the deposits, but now her mind raced with questions.

What was Jackson's connection with her mother? Why would he give her money under the name Jenson Canute, and for what purpose? Why was her aunt's husband talking to her mother? Why? Why?

Until Cassie found the answers, she couldn't face Michelle.

Chapter 8

SPOTTING CASSIE AT the patio table, Sondra made a detour from the path leading to the guesthouse toward the patio. Oreo was belly up asleep on the chair beside Cassie while she was zoned out.

"Hey, girl, whatcha doing?" Sondra's Copper-coloured skin looked silky in the white sleeveless dress that contoured her shapely figure. The dress that rode inches below her thigh was too short for office attire, but no one who valued their hearing dared tell her of her etiquette faux pas. Not that she'd listen. Sondra was her own woman, and there was no swaying her mind. "Earth to, Cassie." Sondra snapped her fingers in Cassie's face to get her attention when she didn't respond to her voice.

Looking up from her iPad, Cassie removed the AirPods from her ears. Aerosmith's Dream On blared from the earbuds. "Sorry I didn't see you there. Doing research."

The late afternoon sun was hot and intense, and the moisture in the air left from the earlier day's rain made the air thick.

"Clearly." Sondra fell into the chair across from Cassie. Her thick, dark hair, combed smooth, haloed the pretty face with almond-shaped eyes daubed with bronze eyeshadow and full cherry-red lips. At her long neck, she wore the gold chain with the heart-shaped locket Olivia and Cassie gave her for her birthday.

"You're home early." Cassie flipped the cover on the iPad and set it on the table.

"I had a dentist appointment, and it's not that early. It's four o'clock."

Oreo stretched out on the chair and followed it with a yawn before giving Sondra an eye over and falling asleep again.

"Shit, I didn't think I'd been out here that long. No wonder I'm hungry." Cassie reached into the chip bag for a handful and held the bag up to Sondra.

Sondra tsked. "Does this body look like it enjoys chips?"

"Um, yeah. I've seen you down an entire bag in one sitting. With dip," Cassie pointed out, and both women laughed.

Sondra reached into the bag and pulled out a handful of chips. "I'll have to work it off doing extra cardio with my honey tonight." Large, dark, smiling eyes winked at Cassie.

Cassie winced. "Christ! TMI. You really should think about using that filter from time to time."

"Where's the fun in not telling you exactly what's on my mind?" Sondra tossed a chip into her mouth and hummed at the experience.

"It's not fun when I can't unsee the images you put in my head. Some images require the analytical mind of a shrink, which I don't have. Besides, you're my tenant, and I demand respect."

"A tenant pays rent, which I do not and don't expect to do so any time soon." Sondra sat and crossed one slender leg over another.

"Yeah, well, don't make me rethink that decision."

"We both know you love me too much to boot Malcolm and me out on our fine asses." Sondra tossed a second and third chip into her mouth.

After the briefest hesitations, Cassie said, "I do love you, but your and Malcolm's stay at the guesthouse may not be long." Cassie told Sondra about Michelle's emails to Olivia and the submission to the court to contest her inheritance.

Sondra sat up in her chair. "That bitch." A remorseful smile followed the words delivered with heated emotion. "Sorry, I know she's your aunt, but she's a bitch nonetheless to take your home."

Cassie nodded. "And the money. I felt the same when Olivia told me she'd been receiving the threatening emails since shortly after Daddy's death."

"I hope you were looking up for a good solicitor on the iPad?" Sondra crunched down on a chip. The tang on her mouth felt heavenly.

"Olivia's doing that. She has been talking to a solicitor who has agreed to fight this on our behalf. But I think a conversation with Auntie Michelle can resolve this crazy misunderstanding. We're family." Cassie flipped the cover on the iPad to show Sondra the screen depicting the articles on Michelle. "I've been reading up on Auntie Michelle. You know, trying to get to know her before I approach her."

Sondra eyed the iPad screen. "Did you find what you're looking for?"

"Some, but only by talking to her can I get to know her. You know?" Cassie set down the iPad back on the table.

"Are you sure that's what you want to do, Cass? I mean, she sounds like a cold, hard woman."

"She does, but it's something I need to do. One minor problem. I can't get past her assistant Kayla to schedule an appointment to see Auntie Michelle."

Sondra bit into another chip and thought a creamy dip was needed. "She is a mucky-mucky and very busy."

"I'm family, goddamn it." Cassie's tone was harsh, and the distress ran across her face.

Sondra let the outburst pass. Sondra had been known to let her temper dominate occasionally and understood the heat of emotion Cassie felt because nothing took hold of you like family. "You are, darling, but you haven't been in her life, and she doesn't know you from Adam. You must give your aunt time to get to know you and let her take you in small doses." Sondra's tone sounded artificial and unalive.

Cassie shrugged. "I know you don't believe any of that."

"Shit, no. Fast and hard is my motto, but that's what works for me. For you, slow and easy is what will work. That sweetness thing you have going, in small doses, might break the ice queen."

Cassie took a moment to think about that. "Maybe you're right."

"Yeah. I am. When have I been wrong?" Sondra asked, and Cassie knew better than to point out the many times she had been. "And you can count on Malcolm and me to help you any way we can."

Cassie's brow raised in interest. "I hope you mean that."

"I do, my darling. After all, my comfortable, rent-free home is at risk. How about you round up Olivia and George and come to my place for dinner? We'll have a barbecue."

"You have food? Barbecue requires meat." At the mention of meat, Oreo woke up and raised his ears. "You know, like steaks, hamburgers, or hot dogs."

Sondra hadn't been shopping for days and rolled her eyes to the sky as she took a mental inventory of what was in her refrigerator. "How about you bring the steaks, the salad, and a hot dog or two along with the buns? I have a craving for a hot dog. Don't go bringing those tiny, cheap finger-size dogs. I'm talking about those long-ass all-beef hot dogs."

At the mention of hot dogs, Oreo woke and barked his agreement, and Cassie let out a snorted giggle.

"It would be easier if you came here for dinner."

"I accept your invitation and tell you what, I'll bring the wine." Sondra scratched Oreo's ears.

"It better not be from Olivia and George's stash. They'll know." Cassie smiled at Sondra when her eyes looked at her obliquely. "Well, I better get busy in the kitchen to marinate those steaks and make the potato salad."

Sondra pushed to her feet. "Fine, I'll help as my contribution to the dinner."

"Um, yeah, you will. I need a potato peeler. Yes, you too, Oreo," Cassie said when Oreo barked.

"Fine. I need to change into comfy shorts and a tank top." Sondra picked up her handbag off the table. "I'll be right back."

"By the way, will Malcolm be joining us?"

"When have you known Malcolm to pass up a good meal? He should be home by six, but I'll text him." Sondra reached into her handbag for her cell phone.

"Good. I have something I need to ask him."

"What do you need to ask him?"

"I want to know if he can hack into the bank system for me. Don't tell anyone, okay." Cassie turned to head into the house, leaving a stunned Sondra staring at her.

Chapter 9

CASSIE SERVED A great meal of grilled steak, vegetables, and potato salad. Afterward, Oliva and George volunteered to clean up.

Night had descended, and the lights in the kitchen beamed bright. The faint smell of grilled meat hung in the air and mingled with brewing coffee. The counters were wiped clean, and the dishwasher hummed as it sprayed dinner dishes and cutlery with hot water.

"You kids, go ahead to enjoy whatever fattening, sugary concoction Sondra has at her place. George and I will stick around here and relax on the patio with a glass of cognac, but remember, no brownies." Olivia hung the damp dishrag on the oven's door handle to dry. She wore comfortable jeans and a loose shirt, and her feet were bare. Her hair was tied into a loose ponytail.

"One, you banned me from making my deelish, medicinal brownies when I moved into the guesthouse, not that this is your place, but I'm a woman of my word. I haven't made a pot-laced brownie in months, which, by the way, is killing me. Two, I understand old folks tire easily, and I'm good with you staying behind." Sondra opened the freezer door and rummaged through the stack of boxes.

"Who are you calling old? George and I are in our prime," Olivia asserted, pouring Hennessy into two snifters. "What are you looking for?"

"A cheesecake, a tiramisu, anything sweet. I knew I'd find something good in here. You don't mind if I take this, do you? Good," Sondra said before Olivia answered and retrieved the red velvet cake from the freezer. "What? You thought I'd have anything dessert-like. I don't even have real food in my refrigerator."

Olivia looked at Sondra and raised her eyebrows. "You invited us to dessert at your place," she pointed out while George and Cassie stifled a smile. Malcolm, knowing better than to comment, remained quiet. He wore a white polo shirt and black chino shorts.

"That didn't mean I had any, only that I would serve it." Sondra picked up the pot of coffee resting on the hot plate. "Come along, Malcolm and Cassie. We have cake and coffee to go along with it. Yes, you too can come," Sondra told Oreo, who stood on his hind legs and rested his front paws on her thighs.

"She's far too shy and should speak her mind more. Don't you think?" George had changed from his work scrubs into khaki shorts, a yellow polo shirt and tan loafers. His hair was tousled, but sexily so.

The night was warm, and the humidity left behind from the morning rain pressed down like a wet blanket. A large white moon sailed in a black sky glowing with stars. The breeze that fluttered carried the scent of the woods, the music of cicadas and crickets, and the gurgling creek.

"She is a handful. That boy must sleep with one eye open, and if he doesn't, he should." Standing by the patio railing, Olivia sipped on cognac and watched Sondra, like a general, lead Malcolm, Cassie, and Oreo to the guesthouse. "You laugh, but I'm serious."

"From a man's perspective, she's the type of wild that makes life interesting. If you know what I mean." George winked at Olivia. "Come sit with me and enjoy this beautiful night and maybe neck a little."

Olivia laughed and took hold of George's hand. "Don't let Sondra hear you say necking. It'll reinforce her notion that we're old folk. But count me in."

At the guesthouse, Sondra thawed the cake in the microwave—one of her few kitchen talents—and set three slices on white china plates. "So, Cassie, now that we're here sans Olivia and George, tell us what you want Malcolm to help with."

"Whatever I tell you, I want it to remain between us." Cassie poured coffee into three white mugs and followed Sondra to the living room. "Malcolm, I may be asking for too much, so I want you to tell me if you don't want in."

The guesthouse was a small, homey bungalow. The avocado green painted walls were covered in splashy art— one of Sondra's few additions. Windows with a view of the grounds were covered with smoke-gray blinds. The floor was blonde wood, the dining room table was dark oak, and the living L-shaped sofa was teal. The kitchen was steps from the living room, with gleaming stainless steel appliances and white cupboards. Beyond the dining room were the bedroom and bathroom.

"You tell us what you need, darling. We're here for you." Sondra set the cake plates on the coffee table.

"Okay, but you really need to keep this between us. I'm not ready to tell Olivia yet. She won't support me bypassing her and our solicitor and going directly to Auntie Michelle. And what I'm about to tell you may compel her to dislike her more." Cassie sat on the sofa and tucked her legs up under her.

Sensing girl talk coming, Malcolm picked up his coffee cup and cake plate, held the smile he pasted on his coffee-coloured face and pushed to his feet. "I'll leave you to talk. Come on, Oreo. We, men, will watch the baseball game in the bedroom."

Malcolm wore a black T-shirt that mapped out a muscular frame, and the faded jeans hugged a tight behind. His eyes were as dark as onyx, as were his short-cropped hair and stubble.

"Sit your ass down, Malcolm and listen. You too, Oreo." Sondra's stare made Oreo whine before he jumped on the sofa beside Cassie.

Cassie clamped her hand on Malcolm's arm. "Stay, Malcolm. It's your help that I need." Malcolm sat back down on the sofa beside Oreo.

"Talk to us, girl," Sondra said.

"There were monthly deposits to my mom's bank account of three thousand dollars that went on as far back as her online account gave me access. So, for all I know, they've been going on for years, but being her account, I couldn't get the information. I only learned about them when she died and was going through her things." Cassie took a sip of coffee from the cup she held between her hands to wet her dry mouth.

"Free money, and that's bad because?" Malcolm stuffed his face with red velvet cake while Oreo rested his head on his thighs, hoping for a taste.

"Shut up, Malcolm." Sondra stared at Malcolm with traces of the cream cheese frosting on his lips and wondered why she loved this man as much as she did. Love was blind and sometimes even cut off your sense of smell, she thought. "Why are you suspicious of these payments, Cass? Maybe it was an insurance claim, debt owed, or inheritance."

Cassie explained they had no relatives, lived paycheck-to-paycheck, and couldn't afford to lend that type of cash, let alone afford life insurance. "Besides, Mom would have told me where the money came from if she had nothing to hide. The transactions referenced the depositor as Jenson Canute and came from a numbered account. That's all I know and my gut...." Cassie turned over her untouched cake to Malcolm when he eyed it.

"Thanks, babe." Malcolm dug in with gusto. "This is good, and I'm sorry, my man, but you can't have any," he told Oreo when he got an imploring look from the dog.

Rolling her eyes, Sondra shook her head. "Go on, Cass."

"My gut tells me there's a lot more to that money that needs looking into. Especially when looking through the pictures of Auntie Michelle with her husband, Jackson, I recognized him," Cassie said.

"I don't understand why that would raise your curiosity. Of course, you would recognize Jackson. He's all over the news. Marrying into the Huntley wealth tends to get media attention, and his photogenic face is plastered everywhere." Sondra gave Malcolm her piece of cake when his eyes shifted to it. He was lucky he managed to transform his gluttonous food intake into muscle.

"You didn't let me finish." Cassie absently stroked Oreo's head.

"She doesn't let anyone finish. Blah, blah, blah, try living with that twenty-four-seven," Malcolm said through a mouthful of red velvet.

"That misguided observation better have come from the sugar high you're on," Sondra spoke calmly, but the eyes fixed on Malcolm projected differently. "Go on, Cassie."

"The payments were made under the name of Jenson Canute. That's the name he went by. The payments stopped a year or so before Mom died. That's when I remembered seeing Jenson or Jackson arguing with Mom. At the nursing home. Where she worked."

A frown creased Sondra's brow. "Are you sure it was Jackson? What would he be doing at a nursing home and arguing with your mother?"

"That's what I'm wondering now, and it was him. Seeing his photograph triggered my memory and reminded me that their discussion didn't look like two people who didn't know each other, as she led me to believe. Thinking back, it looked intimate. You know, like they knew each other." Cassie turned to Malcolm, who'd finally decided to wipe his mouth clean, while Oreo, who'd given up on getting a taste of cake, fell asleep. "This is where you come in, Malcolm. As an IT guru, I was hoping you could help me with the paper trail of where the money came from. I want you to hack into the bank's computer."

Cassie's proposal came as a shock, and Malcolm's eyes widened. "Jesus, Cass, I'm good but not that good. And hacking into a bank's computer is next-level insane."

"You are that good, and you can do it. You helped Olivia get the necessary information to teach her employer a lesson." Cassie reminded Malcolm.

"Shh!" Malcolm covered Oreo's ears. "Don't go around saying that! We agreed no one's supposed to know, and what you're asking me to do is a whole different level of access, criminal even."

"Please, Malcolm, I need your help." Cassie pleaded. "I need to put this nagging feeling to rest. I know there's something there with Jackson, the money, and my mother and I need to know what."

Cassie's cry for help wrapped tightly around Sondra's heart. "Of course, you'll get our help." Sondra pledged before Malcolm could turn Cassie down. "You're going to help her or get nothing in there." Sondra jutted her chin toward the bedroom.

Malcolm sighed, then set his lips firmly. The woman always hit him where it hurt most. "Fine, I'll see what I can do." Malcolm shoved the last of his cake in his mouth. "You know women are the reason erectile dysfunction is a thing."

Part II

The Middle

There's no salve to prevent you from getting hurt.

— M.L. Lexi

Chapter 10

KAYLA PUSHED AWAY from her desk and got to her feet when Olivia charged into Michelle's office. Kayla sat back down when Olivia shot her a threatening look. Kayla had worked for Michelle for over a decade and, in that time, had gone beyond the call of duty for her. However, Family quarrels, especially between women, wasn't a line Kayla was willing to cross.

"Why are you doing this?" Olivia's eyes were unmistakably heated blue when she opened Michelle's office door and burst in.

Michelle looked away from the people gathered at the meeting table to Olivia. "Could you please give us the room please?" Michelle told the group and waited for her staff to leave the office. "You always did have a flair for the dramatic, Olivia."

"My solicitor tells me you refuse to accept his offer to return my share of the money." Olivia looked poised in the lilac pantsuit over a cream blouse.

"I already told you I would." Michelle's blonde hair flowed like shiny, smooth silk around her face, and she looked elegant in the white ruched V-neck dress. Rubies hung from her ears and around her long neck. It was too bad her outer beauty didn't reflect her inner one.

"I just figured if I made the offer through legal channels, it would seem more authentic to you."

"It's not." Michelle's green eyes were cold and aloof, more so than Olivia had seen before.

"Is it so important for you to hurt Cassie and make her feel like an outcast?" Olivia's anger flared.

"It is." Michelle sat back in her chair and crossed her long legs. "I told you I want everything returned. I'm the rightful owner of Huntley Estate and the money. And that girl must understand she's not who she thinks she is. You should tell her that calling me tens of times daily will not tempt me to change my mind or get her an audience with me."

Olivia rolled her eyes. "Audience? Who do you think you are, Michelle? The Queen of England."

Impervious to the slight, Michelle watched Olivia with expressionless eyes. "I'm a solicitor, and I resolve issues in the courtroom." Michelle's calm, even tone gave the impression of a cobra about to strike.

"No, you want to fight this in the courtroom to make it public and humiliate Cassie." Olivia levelled blue eyes to deadpan green eyes. "What happened to you, Michelle? Who hurt you so badly that turned you into this cold, heartless bitch. I remember when you wanted to set off to a third-world country to fight for women's rights and make a difference in their lives. You were thoughtful and caring, and family was important to you."

"The key word is family." Michelle rose and walked to the sideboard, picked up the bottle of brandy and poured two fingers into a tumbler. She didn't offer Olivia a drink. "That girl is not family, no matter how she or you spin it. You're making me dizzy, Olivia." Michelle motioned Olivia to sit in a guest chair to stop her from stalking her office.

Olivia's stern gaze remained peeled on Michelle. "I'm not the passive, let-everyone-walk-all-over-me woman you knew years ago. I will fight you hard if you don't stop your contesting-the-will nonsense."

Michelle brushed a piece of dark fluff off her dress. "I know that."

"How would you know that?" Olivia sat. "You cut ties with me long ago. You don't know me."

Michelle drank brandy and tapped a pinky finger against the side of her crystal glass. "I know the old Olivia wouldn't have thought to show up at my office, burst in during a closed-door meeting and threaten me in front of my staff."

Olivia shook her head. "I'm not threatening you, Michelle. I'm stating a fact, and there are many more where they came from, which you won't appreciate hearing but will if you don't end your witch hunt."

Michelle's training to not express emotion kicked in, and she smiled faintly at Olivia's remark. "Is this girl the daughter you could never have, Olivia?"

The comment felt like a sucker punch to the gut. It took Olivia a quick moment to catch her breath. Why were women such bitches to one another?

Olivia met Michelle's intense stare. "Aside from the fact she *is* like a daughter to me, I promised Bob on his deathbed I'd watch over her, and I will do anything to protect her," Olivia said and saw the comment touched a nerve in Michelle.

The tension hung heavy in the room.

Michelle gave Olivia a reproachful look. "My brother only cared about himself."

"He cared about Cassie, and I do as well. And I will not allow you to hurt her."

"I can see by that steely look in your eyes you mean that," Michelle said, regaining her composure. "Tell your adopted daughter to stop calling. I have nothing to say to her, and she has nothing that interests me."

Olivia stood. "Cassie has the Huntley obstinate nature, and nothing I say will stop her from wanting to reach out to you to build familial bridges." Olivia walked to the door and stopped. "See you in court, Michelle, and be ready to not only lose your challenge but possibly lose half of your firm."

It took all of Michelle's strength to remain unimpressed by the comment that, from the firmness of Olivia's tone, told her it wasn't an idle threat or a calculated effort to rattle. For a long while, Michelle sat silently, reflecting on what Olivia meant.

Chapter 11

THE UNKNOWING AND the lack of response were frustrating, but the scheming was draining. It was, however, what Cassie needed to do after her many calls to Michelle's office went unanswered and unacknowledged.

Drastic times called for drastic measures, and Cassie planned to get a job at Huntley Knut & Associates to gain access to Michelle. Michelle hadn't met Cassie and didn't know what she looked like.

Sondra suggested Cassie approach it from an internship angle and apply to a male solicitor for the job. Sondra told her that a pretty face like Cassie's could easily manipulate a man. Sondra wasn't wrong. The moment Jackson Knut saw Sandy Olsson—as Cassie chose to call herself—he knew he wanted her to intern for him. After an extraordinarily long interview with Jackson Knut, where he eyed Cassie like an eagle at mealtime, he welcomed her to the firm. Sandy Olsson started work on Monday.

"You wanted to see me, Mr. Knut." Cassie stepped into Jackson's office.

The office was modern and masculine, with dark wood, sturdy tables and louvred glass walls. A big hockey fan, Jackson displayed collector paraphernalia on the sideboard and bookcase, and original oil paintings of hockey greats hung from brown walls. The expansive corner office, one floor below Michelle's, was neat and orderly. It was not a surprise to Cassie since Jackson was a persnickety man.

"Yes, come in. Close the door behind you. Have a seat, Sasha." Jackson indicated the guest's leather chair across him.

"It's Sandy." Cassie sat.

Cassie's straight, honey-coloured hair fell around a young face with naïve eyes and a full, pouty mouth painted in soft pink gloss. She wore a teal shirt with the top two buttons undone and a white lace camisole sexily peeked out. A thin gold chain hung from her neck. The tight brown skirt with a slit on the side accentuated a long body with firm curves and showed enough of her toned leg to capture Jackson's attention. The brown pumps she wore made her long legs look longer. That, too, got Jackson's eye.

Cassie spent a fortune on the new wardrobe, and seeing how Jackson ogled her, however creepy it felt, told her the investment was worth it. Sondra was right when she told Cassie that women controlled the tide of life by controlling men through sexuality.

"Yes, of course, it is. My apologies, Sandy." Jackson rounded the desk, bringing the scent of his expensive cologne. He eased a hip onto the desk corner.

Jackson wore a gray suit, a baby-blue shirt and a silk tie, all branded, all very expensive. His blue eyes were mesmerizing, and his handsome face lens worthy. That was all overshadowed by the predatory way he stared at Cassie. That, however, was of no consequence to Cassie. No matter what Jackson thought, she was there for one purpose: to find out about the money deposited into her mother's account and his connection.

"I wanted to welcome you to Huntley Knut & Associates personally." His voice lingered on Knut. "I run my department on an open-door policy. As your mentor, I want you to feel free to speak to me about whatever is on your mind whenever you like, day or night. I am swamped during the day and am happy to make time for you after hours." Jackson's eyes closely watched Cassie cross one impressive leg over another. Inspiring, he thought.

"That's very kind and noble of you, Mr. Knut." Cassie watched the sparkle fill his eyes at the compliment. Sondra was right again. Praise delivered with conviction goes a long way.

"None of this mister business, Sandy. It's Jackson. Can I offer you a drink?" Jackson started to push off the desk when Cassie rose.

"Let me get it for you, Mr. ... umm, Jackson," Cassie corrected herself when he lifted a finger to point out her mistake. "It's my job to ensure you're taken care of."

"Well, thank you, Sandy. I appreciate your commitment. I'll have a whisky."

Cassie refrained from pointing out it was ten o'clock in the morning. "During my summer internship, I aim to learn all I can from you and ensure your well-being is met, Jackson," Cassi said, smiling warmly.

"I have to say, Cassie, your attitude is very refreshing. Yes, it's very refreshing indeed. And I'm more than happy to teach you everything I know." Jackson's words were larded with innuendo that made Cassie want to recoil, but she held her smile.

"Ice or no ice?"

"Neat, please and thank you." Jackson sat on the tan sofa by the built-in bookcase filled with law books. Cassie wondered if he knew their content. "Have we met before, Sandy? You look familiar."

Cassie walked the glass of whiskey to Jackson, and he indicated for her to take the seat beside him. Cassie sat on the chair across from him. "No, we haven't. I'd remember meeting such an impressive man as yourself." Cassie heard Sondra in her head. Keep your face engaged and your lips smiling with every lie. Cassie smiled wide.

Jackson was visibly pleased with Cassie's response. "I understand you start university in the fall but haven't yet decided on a major."

Cassie nodded. "It's why I'm here. I'm leaning toward law, but I'm not yet there. I want to learn everything I can from the best in the field and am willing to start from the ground up if necessary. Something as simple as maintaining your schedule is not beneath me. I believe you learn by doing and following great minds, which you are, Jackson." Cassie raised admiring green eyes at Jackson, and his ego grew tenfold.

Jackson flashed her a smile, dimples winked out. "I'm happy to take you under my wing and teach you all I can."

More innuendo, Cassie thought. "Thank you, but I don't want you to do me special favours. As I said, I would like to start small. Managing your schedule and running your errands will do. You're a busy man, and to make your life as seamless as possible is fine with me."

"That is commendable, and we can certainly start there. I'll email IT to give you access to my calendar. I'll let Mimi know you're taking over my scheduling. She'll be happy to get it off her desk. She has a full plate as is." Jackson drained his glass, and Cassie bolted to her feet and efficiently refilled it.

"Thank you, Jackson, for your confidence in me." Cassie's tone was grateful and deliberate.

"No, thank yous necessary, Sandy. Why don't we start with you joining me in court on my daily appointments? That will give you a good feeling about the law and what it's all about."

To be with the creep in such proximity for long periods wasn't what Cassie signed up for. What her mother was doing with someone like Jackson was puzzling to Cassie. He wasn't the type of person her mother associated with.

But Cassie had to do whatever was necessary to find the underlying reason for his connection to her mother, and she said, "It would be an honour to shadow you, Jackson. I'm grateful for the opportunity."

"I'm grateful to have such a keen, eager, and beautiful student on my team." Jackson stared at Cassie like a predator, eyes its prey at mealtime.

Chapter 12

KAYLA BEGAN CAUTIOUSLY, as she always did when reporting to Michelle about Jackson's carry-ons, which was often. The man's libido was that of a twenty-year-old, and Kayla didn't mind the spying or snitching for Michelle. A man who didn't hold sacred the vows he made to his wife before God deserved to be exposed for the pig he was, and Kayla happily obliged. Kayla wished someone as conscientious as her would have outed her ex-husband for the swine he was when he slept through his restaurant's kitchen staff.

"Jackson has been spending a lot of time with someone new on his staff. A young intern named," Kayla referred to the lined pad where she kept her meticulous notes, "Sandy Olsson."

With a frown, Michelle clicked the staff directory on her laptop. "There's no Sandy Olsson listed on the directory."

Kayla shook her head. "She's unpaid summer staff. Jackson normally doesn't bother to report the intern staff he takes on to HR, and he has Jimmy issue a generic pass card. The interns Jackson hires don't have assigned landline telephones or a desk. Usually, he piles….."

"Them into the spare meeting room to work from there," Michelle interjected, and Kayla nodded. "How often have I told him we deal with confidential information and can't have non-vetted personnel wandering the office and accessing our files?"

Michele's office was cool and comfortable and glowed brightly with sunlight spilling through the large windows and bouncing off the polished wood. The smell of coffee wafted in the air. Outside, the hum of office chatter mingled with fingers tapping keyboards, ringing telephones, and whirring printers.

"You have told him that too often, Michelle." Kayla sounded indignant as a point of support for Michelle's distressing predicament. Sisterhood.

"How many interns," Michelle strung out the word intern, "did he bring on this year?"

"Three." Kayla read their names off her notes. "All are in their early twenties, perky, and very blonde."

As Jackson liked them. The thought was a whisper in both women's heads.

"But he seems to be most focused on Sandy. She's the one he takes to lunch and asks to escort him to court. In my short conversation, Sandy presented herself as rather naïve and demure for a twenty-two-year-old. If you ask me, that's a veneer for the green-eyed vixen that she is. These young women today have no boundaries, no respect for the sanctity of marriage, or themselves." Had Kayla been at her desk, she would have pulled out the prayer beads she kept in the drawer and prayed for Cassie's redemption. Kayla often spent her lunch hour praying for the debauchery she saw daily in the office. Women today were too loose with their mouths and morals. They flashed their assets willingly and indiscriminately.

"What's Jackson been up to with this girl?" At ten-thirty in the morning, Michelle required an infusion of alcohol, and she pushed from her desk to get herself a glass of Absolut vodka. Jackson was the reason Michelle had Kayla keep liquor bottles stocked on the sideboard.

"My contact from Carpaccio Ristorante tells me Jackson's there often with Sandy for lunch, dining and drinking, and carousing together," Kayla editorialized.

"And on my dime, no less," Michelle murmured, drinking deeply.

"I don't know what happens when they leave the restaurant together. I can tell you security check-ins show that on several occasions, Jackson didn't return to the office for some time after leaving the restaurant." Thoroughness was Kayla's middle name. "You know we can always get one of our investigators to keep an eye on him." Kayla looked at Michelle over the rim of the cheater glasses resting on her pointed nose.

Michelle shook her head. "Too risky. Jackson may find out I'm watching him, and I don't want that. For better or worse, he's my husband."

"Yes. He is." Kayla gazed at Michelle with admiring eyes.

Kayla respected a woman who persevered with her marriage and tried to mend fences rather than rush into divorce. She would never have divorced Bartholomew if he hadn't served her with the papers. Women today give up too quickly on everything. They didn't have the resilience of the older generation.

"As always, you've been very informative, Kayla. Thank you." As an afterthought, Michelle said, "Kayla, arrange a lunch in my office for Sandy Olsson and me."

"Are you sure about this, Michelle?" Kayla interjected worriedly. No good would come from the endeavour.

"I am." It was time Michelle turned toward her problem rather than away. "Please set it up, Kayla."

"Of course, Michelle," Kayla said with the puzzled line between her eyebrows deepening.

No good was going to come out of this, indeed.

Chapter 13

IT WAS WARM inside the guesthouse, with heat trapped from the hot summer day. Oreo eagerly gnawed on the bone Malcolm gave him after dinner while Sondra stacked the dirty dishes and cutlery into the dishwasher. Cassie sat beside Malcolm on the living room sofa. Malcolm's legs were stretched out, his sockless feet on the coffee table, and his laptop rested on his lap.

"Woman, turn the air conditioner on. I can't concentrate with this heat." Malcolm was dressed in weekend casual coral shorts and a red polo shirt.

Sondra set the dishwasher on. "Yeah, because the heat's why your brain is mush." The comment unleashed an argument with a torrent of expletives and insults lobbed at one another, and Cassie waited it out.

Opposites in every sense, Sondra and Malcolm fought like cats and dogs, yet they complemented each other. Sondra was an alpha, and Malcolm was laid back. Sondra was an extrovert, while Malcolm was less so. Sondra was six years Malcolm's senior. The shared constant was that they cared deeply for each other.

"Why won't you turn the air-con on, Sondra?" Cassie got no response. "Why won't she turn the air-con on?" Cassie murmured to Malcolm.

"She wants to save money to buy our own house," Malcolm said. "She thinks we're going to lose the guesthouse and end up homeless."

"You will never end up homeless," Cassie told Sondra before Malcolm could signal her to stay quiet. Cassie had kicked off her running shoes and ankle socks, and her bare feet, like Malcom's, rested on the coffee table, ankles crossed. "If you must move, you have a home with us. You can live with Olivia and me in her home or George's. We have options, but it won't come to that. So, turn on the air-con, woman." Cassie's assertiveness got a raised brow from Sondra and Malcolm.

"Okay. Respect to this balsy Cassie, but let's not get crazy. If worse comes to worst, Malcolm and I know we will always have a home with you, Olivia, and George, but we need privacy. You know we're the vocal sort in there." Sondra jutted her chin toward the bedroom.

Malcolm cringed. "Christ, woman. Do you always have to be so forthcoming about everything?"

Wincing, Cassie said, "Filter, woman. Filter."

Oreo remained unmoved. The bone was more interesting than the drama unfolding in the room.

Sondra's mouth tipped at the corner. "You two are such snowflakes, and the air-con is on. It'll get cool soon enough." Sondra walked to the living room with three glasses of iced tea. "Drink this. It'll cool you off. I hear a lot of tapping on that laptop over there. Tell me what you've come up with."

"After scouring Jackson's calendar, Cassie didn't find anything interesting. But then she only had one year's access. Hacking into the bank is way out of my comfort zone and skill level, but I did come up with something that may help." Malcolm tapped away on the laptop's keyboard with skill and speed. "As it turns out, Jimmy, the IT manager at Huntley Knut & Associates, is a fellow gamer. Buttfart69 is the name he goes by," Malcolm said, and both

Sondra and Cassie's eyebrows raised. "He gave me access to a few internal calendars. Jackson's assistant, current and previous interns, and Michelle's."

Opening the front door for Oreo, who wanted to be let outside, Sondra turned to Malcolm. "Enlighten me as to how that's any help."

"Elementary, my dear, Sondra. I have access to the calendars that go back as far back as five years. Calendars are like a timeline of people's lives. People document everything in there. Maybe we can find the penned meeting between Jackson and Cassie's mother, a code of numbers, something to give Cassie a lead. It's a starting point, and we have to start somewhere."

"That's brilliant, babe, and a total turn-on." Sondra leaned down to brush her lips to his. "My honey-pie may just get lucky tonight."

With a slow, curving lip, Malcolm said, "Really?"

Cassie cleared her throat. "I'm still here."

"Since my brilliant man has an in at the company now, you don't need to remain working for that parasite, Cassie, and feel guilty about hiding it from Olivia. You know you won't be able to contain that guilt for long, and you're bound to spill your guts. We need something stronger than iced tea." Sondra walked to the refrigerator and reached in for the bottle of Merlot.

"The man is a leech and old enough to be my father, but he's handsome and charming for someone in his late fifties." Cassie took the glass of wine Sondra offered.

Sondra gave Cassie an odd look. "You did not just say that."

"I need to keep playing the part of the swooning intern because, as Malcolm said, this is just the beginning of my sleuthing."

"I don't want to hear what you do with this man, but you can quit now. Malcolm will get the information you need." Sondra poured Malcolm a glass of wine and set it on the coffee table.

"No, I need to stick around for a bit longer. I'm gaining Jackson's trust, and he's giving me more access to files and internal information that Malcolm's not comfortable asking his friend for." Cassie walked to the front door to check on Oreo and found him on the porch, taking in the night scene. "You going to stay out here or come in?" Oreo didn't budge. "Okay, scratch the door when you want in."

"If you stick around sooner or later, you will come face to face with Michelle, and that won't work out well." Sondra watched Cassie return to the sofa.

"I'm on the floor below her. I haven't seen her downstairs once in my time there. She spends most of her time in court or meetings or running the company. The woman is a dynamo on steroids." Cassie stopped to think. "I'm not sure what it is that Jackson does."

"This tastes expensive," Malcolm said after he drank some of his wine. "I thought you wanted to save money."

"We are. I took it from Olivia and George's stash. They have so many bottles they'll never miss it," Sondra said. With the financial uncertainty lingering over her head, Cassie thought it best she didn't mention Olivia knew about every bottle missing in her wine fridge. "George does have a discerning taste." Sondra clucked her tongue when she drained part of her wine.

"Voilà." Malcolm clicked the calendar on the laptop screen to life. "I feel like Shaggy on Scooby Doo."

Sondra stopped mid-drink. "Why couldn't you think of yourself as Fred?"

"Who's that?" Malcolm filtered his calendar search to five years earlier.

"The handsome leader of the group." Sondra informed Malcolm.

"Pfft, please. You know I'm more the Shaggy or Scooby Doo type," Malcolm said.

Cassie sent Malcolm a quick smile. "I love Shaggy and Scooby-Doo best."

"You're a woman with great taste." Malcolm turned the laptop toward Cassie. "Take a look at this. There's a notation, which I think refers to the three thousand dollars."

Cassie and Sondra turned their attention to the screen. Both saw the 3k notation appearing on the fifteenth of each month for three consecutive months.

"That can mean anything." Sondra sank back into the sofa's depth and sipped Merlot from her refreshed glass.

"It can, but both you and I know that when you're hiding something, you tend to abbreviate entries to make them unremarkable to prying eyes."

Sondra frowned. "That's a big word for you, babe. Do you use abbreviations to make things unremarkable, not to catch my attention?"

"Of course not, babe. I'm an open book and have nothing to hide." Malcolm remained stoned-faced when Sondra looked over at him to get a guilty read.

"Mmm-hmm." Sondra's wary eyes stared back.

"Anyway, I read this 3k entry as three thousand, which is too coincidental not to refer to the three thousand dollar deposits, especially when Cassie said the deposit went through her mother's account on the fifteenth of each month."

"But it only shows up on the calendar for three months. My mom's bank account showed at least seven years of monthly deposits," Cassie said.

"Did you try getting more information from the bank?" Sondra asked.

"Yeah, I did, but my name wasn't on the account, and they wouldn't give me any information. I couldn't press the issue since I needed to take out the little money Mom left through less than legal means once I stupidly told them she had died."

"I wasn't finished, guys." Malcolm tapped on the keyboard. "The curious part is that the 3k entry appears in Michelle's calendar, not Jackson's." Malcolm's observation had Cassie and Sondra straightening in their seats and turning their eyes to the laptop's screen.

"You're right," Cassie said.

Sondra nodded. "He is, and that, babe, is an amazing find."

"Why would Michelle have the entry in her calendar?" Cassie's eyes puzzled.

"You need to get buttface69 to give you access to bank account files, babe."

"It's buttfart69, and are you insane, woman? I was lucky to get what he gave me. Asking, butty, that's what I call him, to give me access to the firm's bank account or accounting files is asking too much of him. He likes his job."

"Malcolm's right." Cassie took the laptop from Malcolm. "I'll go through Michelle's calendar more closely tonight, and maybe I'll find something more substantial and have a better direction of what files I should try to access at work. Thank you, Malcolm. This is a great start." Cassie kissed Malcolm on the cheek.

"It is my IT sleuth." Sondra rose from the sofa to sit on Malcolm's lap. "You are getting lucky tonight."

Malcolm smiled, pleased with himself. "Remember, Cassie, to be very careful. Do not make any entries or deletions to the calendar or click on anything that may raise any red flags," Malcolm instructed before Sondra got to her feet and reached for his hand.

"Come on, Sherlock. Come and find my G-spot. See yourself out, Cassie, and don't forget Oreo, who's probably fallen asleep on the porch. And remember, we get loud quickly."

"I'm leaving." Cassie closed the laptop and ran out of the house, picking up Oreo off the porch with her free hand. "We need to get far away from this sex palace."

Chapter 14

OLIVIA STROLLED FROM the bathroom toward the bed, and George did the opposite. The burgundy satin night robe she wore on top of the lace camisole flowed behind her like a cape. She smelled gently of the floral fragrance of her perfume and filled the room with its scent. Her chestnut hair flowed in waves around her face.

"Cassie's up to something." Olivia reached for the jar of hand cream on her night table. "I know she is."

George stepped under the spray of hot water, a soothing reprieve after his long day at the hospital. No matter how often George delivered terrible news to his patients, it never got easier. Telling the forty-five-year-old mother of three the small cell lung cancer he found gave her six months to live had drained him.

After his wife's nervous breakdown, which led to her hospitalization, George resolved to leave his workday at the hospital and cast his work thoughts aside. "Cassie's twenty-two. They're always up to something at that age, but that doesn't mean it's anything nefarious." He lathered his hair with shampoo.

"She told me she was volunteering at the library. I didn't see her on Tuesday or Thursday when I was there." Olivia dabbed cream on her hands and rubbed them together.

"Maybe it's another library she's working at." George lathered his body with Irish Spring to wash the day off.

"When I didn't see her there, I went to the next closest library, and she wasn't there either. And she's spending too much time with Sondra, which is never good."

George smiled because laughing aloud wasn't what the moment called for. "Malcolm is there to keep Sondra in line."

Olivia, pfft that. "Malcolm has no more control over Sondra than any of us does, and I've known her long enough to say she's a loose cannon confidently." Olivia heard Oreo's bark and walked to the window.

Under the pool of light from the lampposts hemming the walkway, Olivia saw Cassie running toward the house with Oreo chasing after her. Cassie clasped something close to her chest: a book, a box, a towel. There was too much distance between them for Olivia to make out the object.

Cassie was up to something. Olivia leaned a shoulder against the window frame, wondering what. Cassie was gone from seven a.m. to six p.m., Monday through Friday. Where Cassie was and what she did during that time was still a mystery three weeks later.

Olivia promised Bob on his deathbed to become Cassie's guardian, but it was more than caring for her now. Cassie was like a daughter to Olivia, and she loved her. Protecting Cassie and ensuring her well-being was tantamount to caring for her child. Olivia would give her life to protect Cassie—the inexplicable power of a child's presence in your life.

When their parents died, Olivia became a mother and father to her younger sister, Lottie. She was an aunt to Lottie's daughters, Juliette and Lexi. Then there were George's children. Although both were independent adults, they were family. But Cassie was different.

Cassie's mother died young, leaving her teen daughter motherless. Cassie had been fending for herself since then.

When Cassie tracked Bob, the long-lost father, out of financial desperation, he died months later. In her short life, too much death and more hurt than Cassie should have made Olivia feel a fierce need to protect her. Olivia would do anything for Cassie—even keep secrets that would hurt her. Put it down to the mom in her.

"Look. Tell me that doesn't look suspicious." Olivia pointed out the window when George stepped out of the bathroom.

George watched Cassie shushing Oreo when he barked and skulked her way toward the house. "Okay, she is up to something, but asking or pressuring her to tell you what is useless. She'll lie. Cassie will tell you everything when she's ready, as you'll tell her all when you're ready."

"I understand now what Lottie means when she says the girls will be the end of her."

George brushed the hair from Olivia's face as Styx's *Baby* flowed from the speakers. "Do you regret not having children?"

Oliva gave him a soft nod. "For the longest time, my life seemed empty and meaningless. The bickering and lack of love were unbearable, but Bob not giving me the child I wanted devastated me. I thought a child would fill the void." She looked up at him. "I know now not bringing a child into the dysfunction that was my and Bob's life was a good thing. A child should be conceived from love and brought into the midst of it." Olivia walked to the edge of the bed and sat. There was such sadness in her eyes.

"We can try to have a child." George heard himself say without a second thought.

Olivia cocked her head and swept her green gaze over the man who loved her, as she hadn't felt loved until he came into her life. At that moment, she felt the room fill with the most incredible sense of love. It was as if she could reach out and touch it.

"I know you mean that, and as proud as I would be to have your baby, you and I know that ship has sailed. Physically, I'm too old to carry a child, and mentally, we're both past the baby-caring stage."

She felt the warmth of his arms around her. "You know I have connections to OB/GYNs around the country. They can keep their ear to the ground and let me know when an adoption becomes available."

Olivia looked into his eyes and saw the sincerity in them. George was the perfect Olivia needed in a world where her footing had been slippery for the longest time. She felt completely and utterly encapsulated in his love. This man couldn't be more remarkable if she had designed him from scratch. Good things did come to those who waited.

"Thank you, but I have Cassie now, and she's a handful. She's keeping me busy and awake at night." Olivia breathed in the scent of him freshly showered with a dose of Irish Spring.

"If parenting has taught me anything, it's that your children will do what they want, but mostly that things sort themselves out in time. You have to let your children make their own mistakes while offering your support and love so that they feel comfortable coming to you for help when they fail," George said.

"Wise words." Olivia touched her lips to his, leaning her body against his. "And thank you for listening when I need a listening ear."

"Anytime." George brushed back her hair. "You need to focus your Michelle worrying energy on someone other than Cassie."

"What does that mean?"

"Michelle's threat to strip Cassie of her inheritance, but more so of her bloodline, has you on pins and needles. So, you're trying to do your best to put Cassie in a protective bubble that will never come to pass. Livy, you can't shield Cassie from the unavoidable pain that will come to her when the truth comes out."

Olivia tilted her head. "I thought you were an oncologist, not a psychologist," she said as Styx segued into the sentimental sound of Lobo's *I'd Love You to Want Me*.

"Sometimes I'm both." George played his mouth over hers. Her lips were soft and sweet tasting; all he wanted to do was absorb her until she was a part of him. "Thank you for looking as stunning as you do tonight and smelling so good."

Olivia knew he was deflecting, but she didn't care. She never tired of feeling like a wanted, loved woman. No matter what was going on in her life, George was the one constant that sustained her.

"Thank you for not being so obvious as to telegraph what's on your mind." Olivia looked at his HOT FOR YOU boxers.

Laughing, she pulled him into bed with her.

Chapter 15

CASSIE STOOD AT Michelle's office door, her green eyes studying her aunt. Draped in navy silk and gold with her copper-blonde hair tightly pulled back and bundled into a twist that brought out her delicate face, Michelle looked striking. The pointy red patent pumps were Mischka, classy and luxurious. Sitting in the impressive office behind her desk, Michelle looked larger than life, powerful, and as intimidating as Olivia described her. Cassie started to walk away.

"Come in, Sandy." Michelle signalled Cassie to sit at the round table by the large window with a view of the downtown core.

It was a clear, sunny day, and the sidewalks were crowded with men and women trickling out from tall buildings for the lunch hour. Streets burst with traffic that moved as quickly as maple syrup, and lines formed at the hot dog vendor's cart, restaurant, and café entrances.

"I'm interrupting. I can come back." Cassie could smell the sweet floral scent of Michelle's expensive perfume.

"You're not. I've been expecting you." Michelle studied Cassie. She looked striking in a pink pantsuit. Her blonde hair flowed straight around a youthful face painted in bronze and glossed lips. Young, naïve, and impressionable was how Jackson liked his interns, and Cassie fit the bill. "I hope you like egg salad and coleslaw."

"I do, thank you." Cassie scraped a chair back and sat facing the window, and Michelle sat beside her.

Cassie's heart beat thickly. She had waited a long time to get this close to Michelle. Being as close as she was to her aunt felt surreal and extraordinary. As much as Cassie itched to reveal her true self, there was more information to be gathered. And that required time. If Cassie could ask Michelle the questions she wanted answered, her search could go that much faster, but life wasn't black and white.

"Is there anything wrong, Ms. Huntley?" Cassie bit back the urge to reach for Michelle's hand.

Michelle uncapped the bottle of Perrier and poured it into a glass set out by Kayla that contained two slices of lime and two cubes of ice, as she liked. "No. I wanted to meet you since I was told you are undecided between nursing and law."

"Yes, that's right." Cassie followed Michelle's lead, uncapped the Perrier bottle, and poured it into her glass. "I guess Jackson, Mr. Knut, told you."

"No, he didn't." He wouldn't admit he had a young blonde at his beck and call. "I try to keep abreast of my staff." Michelle's words sent a slight panic to creep up Cassie's spine.

Did Michelle know what she was up to, and the lunch was a ruse to smoke her out? Cassie's throat was so dry she could hardly speak. She sipped Perrier in the refined manner Michelle did, but her taste buds didn't appreciate the carbonated taste as much as Michelle's had.

"So, tell me why you're undecided." Michelle daintily nibbled on her sandwich to avoid egg salad from spilling.

"It's first-year university reservations. I signed up for the sciences and took political science and English courses to cover all angles. You know, just in case." Cassie matched Michelle's small bite of her sandwich.

"Well, then, let's see if I can assist in swaying you toward the law. We can never have enough women in the legal field, and encouraging as many young women as possible to pursue law is a passion of mine. There's strength in numbers, and if we're going to break the glass ceiling, we need all the help we can get."

"I one hundred percent agree. I appreciate you taking the time from your busy schedule to share your thoughts." Cassie forked some coleslaw as Michelle had. Being prim and proper was exhausting.

"So, tell me why you're undecided?" Michelle sipped on Perrier.

"It takes years to attain recognition in legal circles, and that's if you're really good. You know, like you," Cassie delivered the sentiment with authenticity. A solicitor, Michelle is trained to detect lies.

"You flatter me, and you're right about taking time to make a name for yourself, but that could be said for any profession. It could be said for nursing." Michelle chased her small bite of sandwich with Perrier while staring at Cassie. Although she hadn't met her until today, something familiar passed between them. "Sometimes we lean toward a profession because our parents lead us in that direction. Is your mother a nurse?" Michelle asked to sway Cassie to speak about her family.

"Yes, she … is." Cassie put on her lying face. "She's devoted her life to caring for people, and I guess I'm following in her footsteps."

"Would you rather have a cup of coffee?" Michelle offered when Cassie picked up her glass, brought it to her lips, and set it back down before taking a sip.

"I would. Thank you. I'll get it," Cassie said when Michelle started to get up. "Can I get you one?"

Michelle shook her head. "Help yourself. There's milk in the mini-fridge below."

Cassie preferred cream, but she presumed saying so would seem vulgar to someone like Michelle. "I take it black with sweetener. Calories are my enemy."

Michelle smiled. "Aren't they every woman's?"

"These are your sons. I believe their names are William and Harry." Cassie eyed the photographs framed in pewter at the end of the sideboard. William and Harry wore the traditional black robe and graduation cap and smiled at the camera, holding their diplomas.

"That's right. Jackson spoke about them to you?" A mixture of pride and love illuminated Michelle's eyes.

Cassie shook her head. "I've heard about them through gossip in the office. Every girl here has their eye on them, and I can see why. They're very handsome."

"Thank you. William is studying law, and Harry chose to go into medicine." The pride in Michelle's voice was palpable. "They're wonderful sons."

Cassie walked to the table and sat. "William doesn't work here in the summer with you or Jackson?"

"Not this summer. I, that is, Jackson, and I thought that since he worked very hard all year, he should take the summer off. The boys are spending the summer in Italy at our apartment in Lago di Garda."

"It must be nice to have a privileged life," Cassie said before scrubbing the thought through her politically correct filter. "I'm sorry I didn't mean that."

"It's true, though. That's why I started the Huntley Foundation, which offers yearly scholarships to over-achievers from low-income families. The scholarship pays for tuition and housing. As an intern at the firm, you can register your name for consideration and be put at the top of the list."

"Thank you, but my mother opened a savings account for me when I was young. Through wise investing, she saved enough to pay for my education." Cassie bit into her sandwich to fill her mouth and keep herself from talking and tripping over her lies.

"I'm sorry. I meant no disrespect. I figured because you're an older student, you postponed your education to earn the money to pay for your tuition. There's no shame in that, Sandy. I hope Jackson is compensating you well. Is he?" Michelle wiped the corners of her mouth with the napkin. The casual, pleasant tone gave Cassie no indication Michelle's jealousy was striking out at the woman she believed was manipulating her husband for money or sex or whatever satisfied her agenda.

"I'm not getting paid." Cassie set the sandwich she wished was a cheeseburger down. "I'm here to learn from Jackson and all the firm offers."

Of course you are. "Well, the offer is there if you'd like to take advantage of it."

Cassie stared at Michelle for a moment, unable to decide whether Michelle was genuine or fishing. "That's very kind of you." Cassie checked her wristwatch. "I really should get back to work."

"Yes, of course. I enjoyed our conversation and would like to pick up where we left off," Michelle delivered the words with a feigned sincerity that would have garnered her an Emmy.

Michelle had only touched the surface. A second, and possibly a third, conversion was necessary to gain Cassie's trust and have her stop lying. People lie to hide guilt, secrets, or trauma. Michelle was sure Cassie lied to conceal her remorse and secrets about her plan to cozy up to Jackson. One way or another, Michelle would find out what Cassie was hiding.

"Sure, that sounds good." Cassie efficiently cleared the table.

"You don't need to do that."

"It's the least I can do since you paid for lunch."

"Thank you. I'll have Kayla schedule another lunch meeting. And remember, my door is always open, Sandy," Michelle said, her eyes following Cassie out of the office.

Cassie's folksy talk and earthy attitude didn't fool Michelle, and she called Kayla into her office. "Keep a close eye on Cassie, Kayla."

Kayla read the request as code for Jackson's up-to-no-good with his intern again and said, "Yes, Michelle. I'll report weekly or more often if necessary."

"Thank you, Kayla. And set up another lunch with Cassie in a couple of weeks."

Chapter 16

GEORGE BRUSHED A dozen ears of corn with his homemade garlic butter recipe with spicy hot sauce and set them onto the heated oiled barbecue grate. The corn required fifteen minutes to cook, giving George fifteen minutes to grill the marinated steaks, hot dogs, and hamburgers. By noon, when everyone arrived, lunch would be ready to serve. George was nothing if not efficient.

The day was hot and dry, and the white polo shirt, cotton shorts, and a Blue Jays baseball cap kept George cool. His eyes were shaded behind dark lenses against the sun that gleamed gold through a clear blue sky. Oreo barked and chased Nibbles, who was having a grand old time teasing his canine friend.

George was against the ruse Olivia orchestrated as a family lunch, but moving mountains was easier to achieve once she set her mind to something. Lottie, her husband Adam, and their girls were due to arrive in half an hour. Sondra and Malcolm would make their way from the guesthouse to the main house before the first steak was served. George's children, Chris and Evangeline, with their significant other, were also invited to the family lunch, a ploy to reintroduce Marco to Cassie.

"I have a terrible feeling about this, Livy." George flipped the corn to sear grill-mark the other side. Presentation was everything. "You couldn't come up with another scheme to occupy Cassie's time and keep me out of it?"

"You're the chef in charge of grilling. Leave everything else to me." Olivia set the plates and cutlery on the table. "Cassie needs a diversion from whatever she's involved in, which I know is nothing good to do with Michelle. Marco is a great distraction. She got along well with him before and will again."

"Yeah, so well, they stopped seeing each other, and you don't know that she's involved with Michelle." George closed the barbecue lid to seal in the heat.

"My gut tells me she is." Olivia's hair was bound into a ponytail. She wore green pleated shorts and a floral linen shirt with green, orange, and white strokes. Olivia's sun-bronzed face looked a healthy glow, and she wore no makeup. "Cassie and Marco are young and don't know what they want."

Rolling his eyes, George took a swig of his beer. "And you do."

"Not necessarily, but Cassie needs a distraction. And what better distraction than a man who's smitten with you? Marco's handsome, funny, polite, intelligent, and, as your protégé, he has a great future." Olivia walked around the table, inspecting the setting to ensure it was perfect. Nodding with satisfaction, she walked back into the house.

George followed Olivia. "Marco is a good guy, and I thought he was perfect for Cassie. It's why I introduced them, but…."

"But nothing," Olivia cut George off. "Cassie needs a distraction because I know she's up to no good."

Cassie walked in on George and Olivia's conversation. "Who's up to no good?"

"Umm … ah…."

"Sondra. The bottle of Pinot Noir I was planning to serve at lunch is missing, and I know she took it." Olivia jumped in when George became tongue-tied. "She thinks I don't know she's been helping herself to our wine bottles."

Olivia uncorked the bottle of Shiraz and Cabernet Sauvignon she chose instead. "I'll have a word with her."

"My money's on Sondra winning the tongue-lashing," George murmured, and Cassie snorted a giggle.

"Cassie, can you please dress the salad? You, George, best tend to the corn, or we'll end up dumping it all. Chop, chop."

"Shit." George sprinted to the patio.

"A brain the size of the universe," Olivia sneered, watching George fumble the hot barbecue lid open.

"So, who's all coming for this lunch of yours?" Cassie poured olive oil and squeezed lemon juice onto the chopped lettuce, sliced cucumber and tomato. Cassie tossed the salad and added crumbled feta and Kalamata olives.

"The family, the wine thief and her drinking accomplice," Olivia said, but there was no malice in her tone. "And…."

"I need a bowl out here, stat," George called out from the patio.

"I'll take it out to him." Olivia volunteered to sidetrack the conversation with Cassie.

"Did you tell Cassie about Marco coming?"

Shrugging, Olivia handed George the bamboo bowl and cold beer bottle she brought him. "She'll find out soon enough."

"This is bound to turn into a great family lunch." The sarcasm rang clear in George's tone.

Oreo's bark rang loud as he bounded onto the patio with Sondra and Malcolm following. Sondra looked summery in a yellow sundress and Roman sandals, and Malcolm wore the body-fitting white T-shirt Sondra picked that traced his toned chest and tan linen shorts. His running shoes were metallic-gold high-top.

"Hey, George, how's it hanging?" Malcolm flashed a bright, white smile.

"Christ! Malcolm, at least pretend to have a smidgeon of class," Sondra said. "How goes the battle, George?"

"It goes. Beer's in the cooler, Malcolm. By the table." George checked the steaks on the grill and shifted them to sear a diamond-shaped grill mark on the meat. "Olivia's inside, Sondra, and a forewarning, she may talk to you about the missing wine bottles."

"It's all her taking the bottles. I have nothing to do with it," Malcolm rushed to say in his defence.

Sondra's dark eyes narrowed. "You're drinking them with me. So you're an accomplice."

"No one is a thief or an accomplice. You're welcome to our wine. It was merely a warning," George said.

Malcolm leaned in and whispered, "You're going to be sorry you said that, George."

Sondra looked over her shoulder with a squinty-eyed look. "I heard that." She continued to head into the house.

"The woman has abnormally good hearing." Malcolm reached into the cooler for a Corona bottle.

"They all do, Malcolm. They all do," George said, and both men sipped beer and mulled that over.

In minutes, the patio teemed with family and laughter. The mouthwatering smell of grilled meat painted the air. Surrounded by so many people, Oreo ran about happily barking as Bob Marley's voice, assuring everything would be all right, flowed from the speakers Malcolm set up.

"Look who I found at the front door." Cassie levelled her eyes at Olivia.

"The fireworks are about to begin," George said to Malcolm. "Good thing we have front-row seats." George tipped the beer bottle to his lips and drank deeply.

Chapter 17

TIRED BUT SATISFIED by the outcome of the family lunch, Olivia popped the cork on the bottle of Krug champagne she hid in the pantry behind the oatmeal canister—the perfect hiding place. Sondra would never think to take oatmeal and would never find the bottle.

"Champagne? What are we celebrating?" George unclasped his watch and set it on the dresser.

"A perfect, uneventful family lunch, o ye of little faith." Olivia poured champagne into two flutes. "Cassie and Marco got along great and made plans for next week."

George kicked his loafers off. "O ye of too much faith."

"What's that supposed to mean?" Olivia returned the champagne bottle to the ice bucket and handed George the flute. Her face had a rosy glow from being under the sun all day.

"You're putting far too much trust on a twenty-two-year-old plotting, scheming girl." The fizz of champagne on his tongue told George it was Krug. "Since when do you find spending money on a bottle of champagne not wasteful?"

On a strict budget for most of her life, Olivia often forgot she had a flush bank account due to Bob's generosity and saved more money than she spent. With the looming threat of Michelle contesting the will, Olivia decided to splurge on the bottle of Krug—less money for Cruella. "Once in a while, you need to treat yourself. You know?" Olivia touched her glass to George's.

"I do, and this is great. What say you we finish it all tonight?" George kicked off his shoes and sat next to her in bed, sinking himself against the mounds of pillows Olivia loved to stack against the headboard.

"I say, it's a plan. What did you mean by Cassie being a plotting, scheming girl? She's not like that."

"Every twenty-two-year-old schemes and Cassie is no exception." George wrapped an arm around Olivia's shoulder, and she pressed closer to him and filled herself with the scent of sweat and man. "You, my love, see everything through a positive lens, and you mostly see the good in people."

"And that's a bad thing?"

Glowing candles filled the room with the sweet smell of vanilla. Beyond the window, stars as clear as diamonds sparkled in a charcoal-black sky with a moon sliced in half.

"Not at all, but sometimes your positive outlook blinds you to the reality of life."

Olivia pulled away from George and looked into his eyes. "What do you think Cassie's up to, PoD."

His lips stretched out in a smile. "You haven't called me Prince of Darkness in a long time."

"Don't deflect. Answer my question, PoD. What do you think Cassie's up to?"

"If I were a betting man, I'd say Cassie told Marco she likes him and would like to get to know him better, but she has too much on her plate right now. Karlee may promise to call Marco when she has a clear head. In the interim, she may talk him to tell you they'd resumed their relationship so you would stop your attempts to hook them up. You know, nowadays hooking up to the kids means…."

Olivia jumped in. "I know what it means, and I'm not trying to 'hook them up.' That's the last thing on my mind."

George's mouth tipped at the corners when Olivia firmed her lips. "Then, like the vixen that is every woman, I'm going on a limb to presume she perhaps leaned close to him and covered his mouth with hers for long enough that he needed to come up for air. Left stunned and staring at her, Marco agrees to do whatever she wants."

Olivia widened her eyes and raised her eyebrows. "You eavesdropped on their conversation."

"More like they didn't check who might be close by when conducting their conversation, and their voices carried to behind the hedge where I stood. And more like I couldn't bail out when they started talking because they would have seen me, and awkward," George said the last word in a singsong voice.

"Along with being a medical doctor, you have always been an excellent spin doctor." Olivia reached for the bottle of Krug and refilled their glasses. "Is that what she said?"

George nodded his head. "Don't look so worried. As I've said to you before, things will sort themselves out. They always do."

Olivia nodded and gave him a small smile. "What do you think she's involved in?"

"I don't know. She didn't elaborate on that."

"I'll get it out of Sondra. She knows what Cassie's up to," Olivia exclaimed with impatience.

"You can, but you won't. Sondra will never be able to keep to herself that she told you, and Cassie will never trust you again." George's eyes did not leave Olivia's face. "Trust is an invaluable commodity you can't afford to throw away on a young woman who needs to rely on you."

There was a small silence before Olivia said, "She's going to find out sooner or later, isn't she?"

George nodded. "However bad the news, it would be best if it came from you."

A terrible feeling of hollowness and guilt settled inside Olivia. "She's not ready."

George's glance rested on Olivia. "Or is it more that you're not?"

Contemplative, Olivia sipped on champagne. "Maybe a little bit of both."

"Far be it for me to lecture, but Cassie's looking for answers, and if she's as stubborn as you are, she won't stop searching until she gets them."

Olivia leaped to her feet and paced the room. "How do I tell a girl who lost the man she believed to be her father and became emotionally attached to that he's not? It would devastate me."

George's eyes followed Olivia, pacing back and forth before him. "Me too, but as much as most of us can't handle the truth, we demand it."

There was a brief pause on Olivia's part. "Why do you think that is?"

"In my profession, people need to make plans, organize their affairs, and make peace with those they wronged and God. In general, I guess, the knowing is better than the not knowing."

"I can't tell her, George. I just can't. It'll crush her, and she's still too emotionally frail from Bob's death." Olivia's throat felt achy.

"You will." George pushed off the bed and walked to Olivia standing by the window, her eyes fixed on the darkness beyond it. George took her in his arms because holding was what she needed. "You will tell her everything when you're ready and sense it's the right time."

"She's going to be devastated." Tears started down Olivia's face, and she pressed her face to his chest.

"Bob used to say that Cassie was a strong girl made of Huntley stock, and I agree. She's been through more than most her age and survived." It'll shock her initially and hurt

her. Denial will follow, but she'll rise and move past it."
George slid his fingers under Olivia's chin and lifted her
face to his. "You will too, Livy. Come on, let's get you in
bed. You've had a long scheming day yourself."

Olivia gave him a teary smile.

Chapter 18

CASSIE STOOD BY the kitchen door and studied Jimmy Star, aka buttfart69, at his desk. He was in his mid-twenties, medium height with unkempt shoulder-length hair and two days of stubble on his face. He wore moss-green cargo pants, a brown hoodie, and white high-top running shoes. The desk he sat behind didn't reflect his messy appearance. It was neat and orderly, with an enormous mouse pad and an oversized computer screen. There wasn't a piece of paper or pen in sight.

Jimmy's fingers efficiently and swiftly tapped his keyboard while his eyes focused on the screen. Jimmy Star was the technical brains behind Huntley Knut & Associates' information technology department and the person Cassie needed to befriend to get the data she wanted. That would be simple enough. In Cassie's survive-at-any-cost days, she mastered the art of the flutter of lashes, which swayed men to do anything asked of them. Add Sondra's man-handling skills, and she would have buttfart69 eating out of her hand.

Cassie's scan of Michelle's calendar uncovered no more "3k" entries than the three Malcolm found. Cassie, however, found notations later that calendar year for three consecutive months for a sequence of numbers she believed to be a bank account. Cassie needed confirmation from Jimmy whether she was right.

"Hi, Jimmy." Cassie moved close to him when he walked into the kitchen to refresh his coffee cup.

Dumbfounded and thrown off balance, Jimmy gaped at Cassie for a beat. "You know who I am?"

"Of course I do. Everyone knows who you are." Cassie said coyly. She wore a red low-cut shirt over a white lace camisole. Her white pleated skirt rode just below her thigh, and the four-inch slingbacks made her legs look inches longer than they were. She smelled sweet, and her blonde hair fountained around her face in waves. "Do you know who I am?"

Jimmy's response was a vigorous nod.

"Can I help you with that?" Cassie took the white cup printed with the red Star Wars logo from Jimmy's hand. Crossing to the pot of stale coffee resting on a hot plate, she sniffed it. "This won't do for you."

Jimmy's mouth hung open. "It won't?"

Cassie shook her head. "I'll make you a fresh pot. While that's brewing, how about I put together a cream cheese bagel for you?"

"Okay." Jimmy jammed his hands into his pants pockets. "Sure."

"Would you like your bagel toasted, Jimmy?" Cassie's wide and generous mouth curved into a sultry smile.

Jimmy took a deep breath, then said, "Yes, but you don't have to do that."

"I don't mind." Cassie set the sliced bagel into the toaster and lowered the lever. I do it for Jackson, and you're as important as he is."

Jimmy gave her a stunned stare. "I am."

Cassie flashed him a sweet smile. "Yes, you are. You work as hard as he does."

"I have a girlfriend," Jimmy uttered, not sure why he did.

Cassie slanted a look over her shoulder at Jimmy. "She's lucky to have someone as smart, hard-working, and handsome as you."

Jimmy's mouth hung open wider, and his hazel eyes went wide. "You think I'm handsome."

"And very smart." Modulate your enthusiasm, Cassie told herself, or Jimmy might detect the hypocrisy of her act. "You know some women are attracted to intelligence. I think there's even a term." Cassie feigned ignorance as Sondra told her to do. Bizarrely, men enjoyed that. So be it if it got Cassie what she wanted.

"Sapiosexuality"

"Look at you being all smart and stuff. Your girlfriend is probably a sapsexual."

"Sapiophile." Jimmy corrected.

"Yeah, that. Here you go, Jimmy." Cassie's bright green eyes curved into a warm smile that arrowed straight to his heart. "You take your coffee with two creams and three sugars, right?"

Jimmy drew his brows together. "Yes, but how did you know?"

"I've paid attention to you, Jimmy."

"Woah. You have?" Openmouthed, Jimmy watched Cassie pour coffee, wondering if this was happening in real life.

"I have." Cassie handed him the fresh cup of coffee. "And I also know I'm not as smart as you."

"You are that and gorgeous too, boot," he exclaimed without thought, and now he couldn't take it back.

To mask Jimmy's awkwardness and avoid trashing the last fifteen minutes of her calculated work on him, Cassie said, "That's sweet of you to say, Jimmy."

"What is it, Sandy?" Jimmy asked when Cassie let out a small sigh.

"I want to ask a favour, Jimmy, but…." Cassie hesitated a beat for effect, ensuring not to overdo it.

"Ask me anything, Sandy," Jimmy said, his tone eager.

"You mean that?"

"I really do." Jimmy's dark, adoring eyes fixed on Cassie.

"I screwed up. Jackson assigned me a task to access something or other for one reason or another. I'm not as smart as you are," she waved a finger to silence Jimmy when he opened his mouth to correct her. "Jackson was talking so fast. Now, I need to figure out what he wants. I may lose my internship." Cassie feigned oncoming tears. Angelina Jolie, eat your heart out.

"No. No, Sandy, that's not going to happen. Not if I can help it." Jimmy's tone was reassuring as they rested on Cassie's teary eyes.

The glow of delight on her face was swift. "You are the sweetest, Jimmy. All I remember from my conversation with Jackson is the numbers and letters he rambled out. I jotted it down." Cassie reached into her shirt pocket, pulled the yellow sticky note, and turned it over to Jimmy. "I think I got them right."

Jimmy flipped the piece of paper open and read. Christ! It smelled of sweetness and her. Jimmy loved the smell of sweetness and her. "It looks like our bank account number, and the sequence of letters and qwerty is his password."

"You are brilliant. How do you keep all those numbers and passwords in your head?"

"I'm not that brilliant. I see the bank account numbers often enough, and as for Jackson's password, qwerty is the most commonly used password," Jimmy said with certainty of the password Cassie guessed to be what Jackson used. "I've told these people a million times that they need to use stronger combinations as their password because even a novice hacker would have no problem accessing their laptops, but do they listen?"

Cassie let Jimmy rant for thirty seconds before she jumped in to say, "Look at you, full of information and wiseness," making him blush enough to overlook the need to correct her misuse of the word. "If it's too much to ask, say no, Jimmy."

Jimmy shook his head. "Nah. I can get you the statements. How far do you want me to go back?"

"I think Jackson said seven years. You're a lifesaver, Jimmy." Cassie reached for his hand and held it between hers. The warmth from her touch shot down to his groin. "Could you load the statements on a flash drive? And, Jimmy, please keep this between us. I can't risk Jackson finding out."

Jimmy made the universal symbol of turning the key in his pursed mouth. "You can count on me, Sandy."

"Thank you, Jimmy, for your help. Send the flash drive through interoffice mail when you get it done."

"I can drop it off at your desk in fifteen minutes." Jimmy volunteered.

"You are a superstar, Jimmy." Cassie left the kitchen, feeling Jimmy's eyes follow her out, and thought Sondra should hold manhandling seminars.

Chapter 19

KAYLA PERFORMED ONE of her favourite duties: spying on Jackson. Seeing Michelle as distraught as she had been since meeting Cassie, Kayla took it upon herself to do a daily office sweep instead of her usual weekly ones. Coincidentally, Cassie was never around when Jackson was out of the office. Or that's what Kayla put down in her reports to Michelle. Cassie could be found at Jackson's desk working on his laptop when he was out.

A young, beautiful, flexible temptress like Cassie must be rid of.

Michelle wasn't a God-fearing woman as Kayla wished her to be. One of Michelle's few failings that Kayla could overlook. Michelle compensated by being a good mother and, regardless of how despicable a man Jackson was, a loyal wife. No matter how many times Jackson betrayed Michelle, she stood by her man. A devoted woman who forgave a man who lacked a moral compass or respect for his vows deserved respect and loyalty.

Conveniently forgetting her husband's duplicity, Kayla reasoned men today weren't what they used to be. Nelson had slept with every woman who worked for him, but Kayla didn't blame him. Nelson was like every man, weak and powerless when it came to satisfying their sexual needs. And when seduced by manipulative jezebels, they couldn't help but give in. Women controlled men's libidos by flaunting their bodies as freely as they did in their suggestive garments to make them do wretched things. Sluts all of them.

Arched in the doorway of Jackson's office, Kayla watched Cassie at his desk for a moment. Focused and efficiently working on his laptop, Cassie wasn't paying attention to the ambient sounds of office life outside the room. The Louvre blinds were drawn open, and you got a clear view of the sun shower raining over the city. Raindrops pattered on the windows and sluiced down in a long, tear shape.

Sensing Kayla's eye on her, Cassie flipped the screen to Jackson's expense report. "Hi, Kayla."

Kayla looked like her staunchly professional self in a navy blue suit against a cream-coloured tie-neck blouse. Her thin lips were painted soft pink, and except for a light layer of foundation to smooth the lines around her eyes, she wore no makeup.

"I'm sorry to interrupt, Cassie."

"You're not interrupting. I'm just recording Jackson's monthly receipts into his expense report. How can I help you?" Cassie rose and gathered the stack of papers into a neat pile. She wore a waist-high black jacket over an A-line dress that rode to her knees and slingback shoes. Her hair was pulled back, held in place with a black bow at the nape of her neck.

"Since I ran into you, I wanted to check if you're available for a lunch meeting with Michelle on Friday." Kayla smelled the musky scent of Jackson's cologne that lingered in the air. She cringed.

"I don't have my schedule handy, but whatever I have on can wait. If the boss-lady wants to meet with me, she gets priority."

Liking Cassie's response, a thin smile crossed Kayla's lips. "Good, noon this Friday it is. Don't be late."

"Do you know what the agenda for the meeting is? So that I can prepare," Cassie said when Kayla started to walk away.

Kayla shook her head. "Just show up. I'll send you an email invitation." Kayla walked away when she caught sight of Jimmy from the corner of her eye and followed him to his desk. "Jimmy, I'd like to speak with you."

The routine of Jimmy's job kept him from avoiding Kayla and feeding her with what she asked of him. But here she was at his desk, making it hard to shift the thought to the back of his mind. "What is it?"

"I'm checking in to see what you have for me. I haven't heard from you in a couple of days," Kayla murmured to keep prying ears from listening.

Jimmy slipped Kayla a folded note. "That's all I have." Jimmy tapped at his keyboard to avoid eye contact with Kayla.

In his usual unprofessional garb of jeans and hoodie, topped with the shock of the dark, unkempt hair, Jimmy disappointed Kayla. Add to his unkempt appearance his insistence on wearing noise-cancelling headphones in the office, and Jimmy was an absolute letdown. Dressing for success was an out-of-date notion to today's generation. Kids today took nothing seriously.

"Thank you, Jimmy. I'll add this to my report." Kayla kept her voice to a whisper and covertly slipped Jimmy's note into her jacket pocket. "Keep up the good work."

"If you don't mind, I need to run several reports for Michelle." Jimmy lied, hoping to dissuade Kayla from sticking around a minute longer. Kayla was known as the office narc, and associating with her would make him narc adjacent.

"If you're working on something for Michelle, I won't keep you. Make sure those reports are perfect," Kayla said in a raised voice for all to hear.

"Yes, Aunt Kayla, they will be," Jimmy murmured, his body sagging.

Chapter 20

JIMMY DELIVERED THE flash drive to Cassie in the promised fifteen minutes. Kayla's unexpected appearance at Jackson's office left Cassie uneasy, and she waited to get home to open it.

With dinner out of the way and Olivia offering to clean up the dishes, Cassie headed to the patio with her laptop and Oreo. "Go on, Oreo, do your thing. Don't go far. It's getting dark." Cassie seated herself at the patio table and turned on the laptop.

The evening was peaceful and serene, with the sounds of nature preparing for the nightlife: crickets and grasshoppers chattered, and croaking frogs came to life. Toward the horizon, the descending sun lit the sky with a warm orange glow like a burning forest fire. The air was cooling, and the fragrant scent of lilac and roses perfumed it.

Cassie inserted the flash drive into her laptop and clicked the file. Seven bank statements appeared on her screen, and Cassie clicked the first one open. Cassie sat back, quietly observing the screen. There were so many lines of numbers, dates, and transactions. Cassie went cross-eyed. Numbers were her enemy.

Deep in concentration, Cassie's mind was miles away, thinking of numbers and hoping to connect the dots. Cassie's thoughts rolled between questions of who paid the three thousand dollars and why. What was Michelle's role in the payment? Why had her mother accepted the money, and what was Marilyn trading in exchange for the three thousand dollars? No one gave free money. More importantly, what was Jackson's role?

Cassie could ask Jackson, but knowing him as she did now, she knew he'd lie to her. Round and round around the mulberry bush she went.

At least Jimmy was in her corner.

Focused on the laptop's screen, Cassie didn't hear the door slide open until Oreo's bark greeting Olivia and Marco, who stepped onto the patio, broke Cassie's concentration.

Cassie closed the laptop and pivoted to them. "Hey, Marco."

"Hey, Cassie." Marco scratched Oreo's head when he rose, his front paws extended on Marco's legs and his tail swishing in excitement. "Hey, Oreo. Good to see you too, buddy." Marco picked up Oreo to let the dog lick his face.

Marco Tuccillo wore jeans, a light blue T-shirt under a plaid shirt, and running shoes. His five-ten frame was lean, and the dark eyes behind the black-framed glasses intelligent and wise for his age. His nerdy good looks embodied cavernous dimples, neatly combed, short, glossy brown hair, and a freshly shaved face. He smelled of his musky soap.

"Marco popped in for your weekly meet-up." Olivia scratched Oreo's head. "I don't even exist to this little bugger anymore. Do I, Oreo? Remember me? I'm your mother." Oreo responded with a sly smile and a lick to Olivia's face. "Hmmm, just like a man trying to kiss up after deserting the woman who loves him."

Marco let out a hearty laugh. "Not Oreo, because you're a good boy, aren't you, buddy?"

Oreo lapped his muzzle once and yawned.

"That's me told. Can I get you a beer, Marco?" Olivia offered.

Marco shook his head. "I'm scheduled to work at the hospital at one a.m., but a cup of coffee will hit the spot."

"I'll get it." Cassie started to get up from her chair, but Olivia put a restraining hand on her shoulder, and she sat back down.

"I'll get it for Marco, along with a hot veal parmigiana panino with a side order of salad. You could use some meat on your bones." Olivia patted Marco's flat belly.

"That sounds great." Marco raised his glasses on his nose. "I can't remember the last time I had a good, homemade meal. Thank you, Olivia."

"My pleasure, Marco." Olivia scraped the chair back. "Sit down and enjoy your visit with Cassie. I'll be right back."

With a raised brow, Cassie watched Olivia walk away. "She knows."

Marco set Oreo down and watched him set off across the patio and lawn. "Knows what?"

"Our arrangement."

"What makes you think that?"

"Didn't you hear what she said? 'Marco popped in for your weekly meet-up.'" Cassie mimicked Olivia's voice.

"But I did pop in for our weekly meet-up, and all I heard was a hot veal parmigiana panino with a side order of salad." Marco laughed nervously when Cassie shot him a long, penetrating stare. "Sorry, but I'm a resident doctor living on potato chips and energy drinks."

"Yes, of course, I'm sorry." Cassie closed her hand over his. "And I'm sorry I forgot about our standing weekly meet-up."

"No need for apologies." Marco couldn't hold a grudge against the woman he was smitten with. "What were you so focused on when we walked out?"

"I don't want to bore you."

Cassie had changed from the Jimmy-attention-getting seductive attire to pink leggings and a blue patterned flowing shirt, and her feet were bare. Her blonde hair was twisted into a single long braid. Forgetting about her meet-up with Marco, Cassie had washed off the makeup from her face, and Marco thought she looked like a goddess.

"I'm your cover or accomplice, so don't you think you should tell me what I'm helping you conceal." Marco kept eye contact with Cassie, and it took all his strength not to reach out and tuck the loose tendril behind her ear. "You can tell me anything and trust me to keep your secret."

Cassie mulled the idea over, and, deciding she could trust Marco, she told him the Reader's Digest version of her story. "I was reviewing the statements Jimmy downloaded for me when you walked through the doors. I don't do well with numbers."

Olivia walked out with the food tray and set it on the table. The aroma of the spicy tomato sauce had Marco's mouth-watering and Oreo running back to the patio. "Thank you, Olivia. That looks great." Marco dug into his food, savouring and humming in appreciation.

"You're welcome any time to enjoy a great meal at Chez Olivia, Marco. Better yet, I'm pencilling in you to join us for dinner on your nights off. I won't take no for an answer. Now, George and I will retire to our room to watch television. Don't get into too much trouble." Looking suspiciously at them, Olivia picked Oreo up and headed into the house. She turned the patio lights on before disappearing.

"Did you see the look in her eyes? She knows," Cassie said.

"If you say so," Marco said through the mouthful of divine veal.

"I do say so." Cassie stared at him. Tomato sauce stained the corners of his mouth. If he didn't have that good-looking, nerdy vibe, she'd be put off. Besides, sweetness and honey were what it took to get them to do what you wanted. Sondra's words popped into Cassie's head. "As I told you, I'm not very good with numbers, and these statements are full of them. You, being a doctor with a brain the size of the universe, are probably great with numbers."

Marco sighed and pushed his plate aside when those large green eyes stayed on his face. "Let's look at these statements."

Cassie fired up the laptop and clicked on the first file. "It's in Excel. I don't know Excel well, and there are so many lines of entries."

"The date of the deposits in question is the 15th of each month, right?" Marco searched for the date when Cassie nodded. "Oh, and don't use that flutter-of-the-lashes-helpless-look on me. It doesn't work."

Cassie kept her voice low when she said, "I'm sorry. It worked on Jimmy."

"Mmm-hmm." Marco pushed his glasses in place when they slid down his nose. "Not all of us know Sondra as well as I do. That's who told you to act helpless and adorable, right?"

Cassie bit back the smile. "This is my mom's bank account number."

"There are no three thousand dollar payments to your mother's account, but I don't think this is a personal bank account. This looks more like the firm's business account."

"What makes you think that?"

"First, there are too many monthly transactions, mostly credits, with varying amounts to different businesses. A personal account has payments for property taxes, utilities, and such. However, all these payments appear to be inconsequential amounts. Look, five hundred dollars, three hundred, seventy-five, for a firm that size, these are, as I said, inconsequential. But then, there is this." Marco turned the laptop toward Cassie. "It's a recurring transaction that takes place monthly to a numbered account for nine thousand nine hundred dollars."

Cassie shrugged. "Why is that curious?"

"Maybe it's nothing, but transactions under ten thousand dollars keep you from federal scrutiny and maybe from internal checks. Two, it's made randomly to a numbered account as if they're trying not to raise attention. Another sign that tells me that whoever is making the transfer wants to fly under the radar." Marco reached for the panino and took a big bite.

"See, you are smart. I would have never caught that."

Marco swallowed. "What did I say about sucking up?" With his free hand, Marco clicked open the remaining six files.

Cassie watched Marco merge the files, which became hundreds of data lines. Seamlessly, Marco sorted and searched, and when he arrived at the information he wanted, he highlighted it with the mouse.

"See the random pattern, which is not that random if you know what you're looking for?" Marco forked salad.

"Christ! Even this salad dressing is incredible. Olivia needs to bottle this stuff."

Cassie cleared her throat. "Focus, Marco."

"Yes, sorry. It's been so long since I had good food. You know, I think I'm taking up Olivia's offer and will be here often for dinner."

"Sure. Okay." Cassie snapped her fingers in his face. "Focus, Marco."

"Yes, anyway, these under-the-radar transactions go on for months on rotation. One month, it's three transactions and the following two. Then the number of transactions is reversed the following two months, so it becomes two on opposite days and three the following month and so on. The total amount transferred is just under two million dollars, and that's only what I see on these statements. This could be going on for years or possibly still. Unfortunately, the account the deposits are made to doesn't match the sequence of numbers you found in the calendar."

"What does this mean?"

"Give me a second." Marco typed on the keyboard. "I thought it was Switzerland, but it turns out to be the Cayman Islands."

"What are you talking about?"

"The prefix of the bank account to where the payment is made pertains to a Cayman Islands account." Marco pointed to what his search on Google rendered, and Cassie read.

"Are you saying Auntie Michelle is embezzling money from her firm?"

Marco shrugged. "I can't say for sure. This is my first pass at this, and I'm not a forensic accountant, but I know nothing good comes from depositing money into a numbered account in the Cayman Islands."

"Christ! This is too much intrigue for me. All I wanted to do was find out who was paying my mother the money, why, and Jackson's connection to her. Now, I don't think I ever will." Drawing in her knees, Cassie circled them with her arms and pressed her face into them. "I give up."

"No, you don't. It's not the Cassie I know. This is only a glitch. I'll help you when I can, where I can."

Cassie raised sombre eyes to him. "You will."

Marco nodded. "I'm not the numbers expert you make me out to be. Numbers weren't my forte. It's why I became a doctor, but I'll help you with what I can. I know this is important to you."

Cassie felt her heart swell with emotion. Her mother was right when she said: When you least expect it, that meaningful someone comes into your life, and more often than not, he's been there all along. "Thank you, Marco."

The moon shone bright, casting a silver haze with long shadows in the woods and over the land.

"You're welcome." Marco closed the laptop. "Now, what say you to us walking around the grounds to clear your head? Doctor's orders."

Cassie looked into the eyes tenderly, gazing at her. Her steadied breath and expressionless face gave away none of the emotions Marco stirred in her at that moment. Cassie opened her mouth and closed it swiftly.

Cassie thought some more.

Cassie's life was complicated enough without adding the complexity of a man. But Marco wasn't just any man. Marco saw her for who she was and accepted her without judgment. And wouldn't it be great to have a good man who cared for her as much as Marco did on her journey to discover where she belonged?

Cassie leaned into Marco and glided her lips over his, sending a pleasant, shocking ripple reverberating. "That sounds wonderful, doctor. But I have a better idea."

Cassie's glistening green eyes made his heart beat thickly. With a small air intake, Marco asked, "What are you thinking?" although his somersaulting stomach said he knew what was going through her mind.

Rising, Cassie reached for his hand and started to walk him into the house, but he held her back. "Are you sure, Cassie?" He slid his fingers under her chin. "You mean more to me than a passing romance. You make me feel alive in a way I never knew was possible. I've never felt this way about anyone before," Marco said in a strangled voice thick with emotion.

Cassie looked into Marco's eyes. "I'm very sure," she said, taking his hand in hers and holding it tightly as she walked him into the house and, hopefully, to the beginning of an incredible journey together.

Chapter 21

OLIVIA HELD SNOOZING Oreo on her lap while sitting on the bedroom window's ledge. Oreo kept her company the entire hour that Olivia sat on the ledge with her eyes peeled out the window on Cassie and Marco. Olivia's snooping paid off.

Olivia shushed Oreo when instinct kicked in, and he woke to bark at the shadows running across the driveway to the car. "Let's not wake George," Olivia whispered.

Olivia leaned closer to the window and listened for the start of the car. The driver instead put the car in neutral, and the second person pushed it to the end of the driveway to avoid making noise and attracting attention. Olivia deduced Cassie was the one who came up with the scheme because Marco didn't have a duplicitous bone in his body.

"Do you see that, Oreo? That's a man who keeps his promise to the woman he loves." Olivia and Oreo watched the car drive away with the headlights off, and Olivia smiled. "That Oreo is a man who will do anything for the woman he loves."

"What are you up to, Olivia?" George said, shifting in bed and rubbing the sleep out of his eyes. "Come to bed."

Olivia turned from the window toward George. "I'm sorry for waking you." She kissed Oreo's head, set him down on his bed by the fireplace, and walked to the bed.

George eyed the display on the clock radio on the night table. "It's past midnight. Why are you still up, Livy?"

Olivia slid into bed and propped herself on her elbow. "Marco and Cassie have been together all this time."

"Congratulations. Your plan worked." George yawned. "Now, let's get some sleep."

"No, George, you're not hearing me. They were together," she said, her eyes widening to convey the deeper meaning of her words.

George winced and pushed himself to a sitting position on the bed. His hair was sexily mussed, and his chest bare. "Thank you for putting the image in my head, Olivia." Now, I'm wide awake. You've been spying on them all night?"

She turned the night table lamp on and sat beside him in bed. "I'd call it concerned parenting."

"Let's call a spade a spade. You were nosing around."

"Potato, potahto. Anyway, could you speak to Marco?" Olivia's hair flowed loose around her face in a nut-brown wave.

"About what? By the way, you look great. Is that a new nightgown?" George said of the white lace nightgown that set off her olive skin.

"Thank you, and yes, it's new. Now, stop interrupting. As much as I know Marco's in love with Cassie, he's her first. You must speak with him to ensure he doesn't hurt her."

Smiling faintly, George nodded as he said, "No."

"But you said Cassie's like a daughter to you."

"She is, but first love or not, you must let the relationship, friendship, or whatever they have going run its course. A broken heart is part of life and a learning curve. What doesn't kill you makes you stronger, stronger."

"I didn't know you were a Kelly Clarkson fan."

George gave Olivia a long look. "Is she related to the German philosopher Friedrich Nietzsche?"

Didn't she feel stupid? Luckily, he looked good bare-chested, and the feeling quickly passed. "Never mind." Olivia sank back against the bed pillows. "When I say Marco's her first, I didn't mean her first love." Olivia widened her eyes and raised her brows.

It took George fifteen seconds to get the gist of her meaning. "Jesus, Livy, we're not girlfriends, and I didn't need to know that." George gave Olivia a distressed look.

"You're a doctor. Surely, the facts of life should be of no consequence to you."

"It is when it pertains to someone I know and love as a daughter."

Olivia slid closer to George and curled his chest hair, flecked with gray, around her finger. "All I'm asking is for you to talk man-to-man with Marco. Like the talk, a father has with the potential suitor of his daughter."

"No."

"Cassie is smitten with Marco and needs time to fall in love with him. That may not happen if things become strained before she realizes she's in love with him too."

"No." George didn't hesitate to say again.

"Please, George. Cassie's had so much hurt and pain in her life. The last thing she needs is a broken heart." Olivia's big blue eyes softened.

"Don't give me that pouty look from the Sondra Coleman playbook. It's not going to work on me." George pulled Olivia in and wrapped an arm around her. "You underestimate Cassie. She's wiser than most twenty-two-year-olds. It happens when life throws you so many curve balls. Cassie doesn't make decisions without giving thought to what the outcome is."

Olivia's blue eyes were thoughtful as she considered. "You're probably right."

"If anyone should speak with anyone, it's you with Cassie. You should have a motherly talk with her if this is her first time. You need to press on contraception use and the respect a woman should harbour when delving into a physical relationship."

Olivia pulled back, her face beaming with the idea that hadn't dawned on her. "You're right, but I must figure out how to approach it. I can't let her know that I know that she and Marco, you know." The idea came to her. "I know. I'll pretend I know nothing as if it's a mother sharing words of wisdom." Olivia droned on, and George lay face down in bed, covering himself with the pillow to drown her out.

Chapter 22

A JAZZY TUNE drifted from the restaurant speakers over the heads of the Friday after-work dinner crowd dining on carpaccio di manzo, risotto, and drinking martinis. The smell of garlic and roasted meat blended with the scent of expensive perfume. Salmon-coloured tablecloths and vibrant art hung on the exposed red brick walls, and the floor was blonde wood. Servers wore white pleated shirts and black pants. Tres chic. Between the clanging of silverware on China and ice clinking on glass, the chatter of business talk from suited men and women was heard.

Jimmy sat back in his chair and took in Carpaccio Ristorante, a five-star Italian eatery in the heart of downtown Toronto. "Sick, Sandy. I've never been to such a bitching restaurant." Jimmy wore his customary faded jeans with a white T-shirt and high-top running shoes. He did not assimilate with the black credit card crowd.

"You'll like the food even better. It's my thank you for helping me out of a bind." Cassie's blonde hair fell straight down her face. In a white Prada silk suit with gold buttons and a skirt that rode above her knee, Cassie fell right in place with the dinner crowd.

"You don't have to do this, you know." Jimmy sipped on the wine Cassie ordered and felt the party in his mouth, as he never had. He tamed his reaction so as not to give his commonness away. "I'd help you just by asking."

"Will you, Jimmy?"

"Of course, Sandy." Jimmy reached for a pumpernickel roll when Cassie passed him the breadbasket.

"There's butter on the dish under that silver dome."

"Classy," Jimmy said as the waiter came for their food order.

Cassie ordered the veal scaloppini and Jimmy the wedding soup, garlic bread, cheese ravioli, and an eight-ounce steak. He told the waiter to serve it together.

Jimmy said when the waiter was gone, "How do you know about this place? I've worked at the firm for two years and didn't know this restaurant existed." He slathered his bread with the freshly churned butter.

"This is Jackson's go-to lunch place. He's brought me here a couple of times." Cassie saw Jimmy's gaze move around the room as if avoiding eye contact. "What's wrong, Jimmy?" Jimmy took a long sip of wine. What is it, Jimmy? Whatever it is, you can tell me."

"Jackson has a reputation as a player." Jimmy stuffed his mouth with buttered bread.

Cassie played the innocent. "What do you mean?"

Jimmy chewed and swallowed. "I'm not a gossip."

Cassie closed her hand over his. The woman always shot an electric buzz through his system. "Jimmy, it's me. Gossip away to your heart's content. Feel free to say anything that's on your mind."

The smile on his lips bloomed. "You're easy to talk to, not like those conceited, bossy interns who think the world revolves around them."

A faint flush of guilt coloured Cassie's cheeks, and her smile fluttered some, but she pushed on. Cassie was on a mission to uncover the truth. "Thank you, Jimmy. What was it you wanted to tell me about Jackson?"

Jimmy looked to his right and left to ensure no eavesdropping ears. Deeming the coast clear, Jimmy said, "Jackson is known for his roving eye and taking his interns to lunch if you know what I mean. Our place is rife with rumours that escalate into full-blown Mexican novellas." Triggered by his Aunt Kayla, but Jimmy kept that to himself.

"I see, and am I becoming the lead female in this summer's novella?" Cassie bit back the smile when she watched Jimmy's eyes, looking for somewhere to settle. "Well, I can confirm to you that whatever rumours you've heard, they're that, rumours. The man is old enough to be my father and so not my type. I'm here to intern and make it through the summer until school starts. I'm leaning toward a career in nursing, but I'm not settled on it and thought I'd get some insight on the law."

"You're not going to learn much from Jackson. Michelle would have been the better mentor. She's the best in the field."

"Is that so?" Cassie nibbled on the bread stick she picked from the bread basket. "I haven't met her yet. What's she like."

Jimmy chased the bite of bread with wine. "She's smoking hot, but a real bitch, in a capable kind of way. You know? I guess, being a woman prosecutor, she has to be. She's competent at managing the firm and has the most billable hours by far."

The waiter approached their table and picked up the bottle to refresh their glasses. Cassie stopped the waiter from refilling her glass and ordered coffee. The only drunk person at the table would be Jimmy.

"This is a great wine." Jimmy took half of his glass in one swallow.

"Enjoy! There's more where that came from," Cassie said. "It sounds as if you're a Michelle admirer."

"It's more that I feel bad for her. Everyone knows what Jackson does behind her back. As accomplished as Michelle is, none of us understands why she clings to that loser. She has a respected name, is intelligent and beautiful, and runs a successful law firm. With all that going on, she can't shake Jackson. He's like an albatross around her neck, and all he does is drain the company of money and sleep around. Everyone has weaknesses, and I guess Jackson is Michelle's. If I did to my girlfriend what he does to Michelle, I'd be talking with a very high voice."

Cassie laughed at that. "Respect to your girlfriend."

"I can't remember the last time Jackson put in a decent amount of billable hours. Mostly, he drains the company's resources and money. Jackson loves to live the high life and…."

The food arrived. They were quiet while it was served, and the waiter refiled Jimmy's glass for the third time.

When the waiter left, Cassie said, "And what, Jimmy? Tell me so I can defend myself if I have to."

"Rumour has it that Jackson's fathered a child or two with the women he had affairs with and is paying them for their silence. It's why it surprised me he asked you to review his account."

As dumbfounded as Cassie felt, she remained stone-faced. Cassie assumed the account number she found in Michelle's calendar was hers, but Jimmy telling her it was Jackson's drove a hand grenade to her system. It was why Jimmy didn't question her when she requested the statements. He didn't have reason to.

A new set of questions rolled into Cassie's head. Her mouth was dry.

Was Jackson paying her mother hush money to silence her for an unexpected pregnancy—her? Was Jackson her father? Cassie didn't expect that.

None of this made any sense.

Why would her mother tell her Bob Huntley was her father? Why would Bob let her think she was his daughter if she wasn't and take her in when she showed up on his doorstep? Why would he leave her the money and Huntley Estate if she weren't his daughter?

Christ! Cassie was more confused than ever.

"Well, I didn't find anything duplicitous aside from business transactions," Cassie said when she found her voice.

"Really? That's strange." Jimmy slurped the last of his wedding soup. "This is a great soup."

"I'm glad you're enjoying it, Jimmy, but tell me why you find that I found nothing questionable strange."

Jimmy moved on to the cheese ravioli dish and garlic bread, but only after gulping wine. "Michelle had asked for those statements a few years back. Seeing my digital footprint on the system when I downloaded them for you reminded me."

Cassie got a curious line between her eyebrows. "That doesn't seem an extraordinary request. It's her company, and I assume, as the president, that appraising the company's statements is routine. It's her right to see what's going on with her money."

"True that." Jimmy reached for another slice of garlic bread and took half in one bite. "The interesting part is that when Michelle had me follow the paper trail, in confidence, by the way, I discovered the account was set up at Jackson's request." Jimmy filled his mouth with creamy ravioli, and Cassie patiently waited for him to chew his food and swallow. "Jackson can't make such requests willy-nilly, let alone use it to pay his expenses and only his. He may be a partner, but Michelle is the firm's owner and the only one who can approve new accounts. She hadn't approved it, and the VP of Finance knew nothing about it." Jimmy let out a quiet belch. "Excuse me. You think I can have another glass of wine?"

"Are you sure, Jimmy?"

"Yes. I'm pretty sure I'd like more wine."

"No, Jimmy. I mean about the account thing." Cassie caught the waiter's eye and ordered a glass of wine. "This is the last glass. Have more garlic bread, Jimmy, to soak up the alcohol." Cassie aimed to get him a little drunk to get him talking, but Jimmy was now verging on blotted. "Do you know if Michelle found anything questionable?

Jimmy shook his head. "I don't know. My role was to provide her with the account info, but I know something about Jackson Michelle doesn't. I'm IT. I'm like a priest in the confessional. I get to see everything that goes through our system. I'm like a digital God." Jimmy waved his hands in the air to encompass the room, but it looked more as if he was swatting flies.

"I know you are. Let me order you a coffee." Cassie signalled the waiter to bring a cup of coffee. "What do you know, Jimmy?

"Jackson has," Jimmy's brain muddled, he groped for words, "An account in the Cayman Islands. I've seen the email correspondence. You know who has an account in the Cayman Islands?"

Marco's comment flashed in Cassie's head. "No, who?"

"People who embezzle company money, that's who." Jimmy was starting to slur his words. "What are we having for dessert?"

Jesus! The man was a bottomless pit. "We'll order dessert in a minute. Before we order, one question."

"Shoot."

"As a law firm, I assume we save emails for years," Cassie said.

"Yeah, we do."

Cassie gave him a half-smile. "Could you do a deep dive into Jackson's emails, personal and business, without leaving a paper trail, telling anyone, or asking me why I want you to do it?"

"Yeah, sure, anything for you, Sandy." Jimmy's clouded mind floated. "My girl would love this place. It would blow her mind if I brought her here, but I'm not sure I can afford it."

Cassie encouraged Jimmy to drink coffee. "Set a date with your girlfriend. I'll make the reservations. It's my treat. I won't take no for an answer, but you must take credit for it. Otherwise, it won't work out well for you. Trust me."

"I do trust you. Nicola's birthday is coming up, and I'll forever be her fave IRL character if I brought her here."

"It's set. You'll order whatever you want for Nicola, and I'll make sure they pour you the best champagne and present her with a beautiful birthday cake. Plan to treat her like a queen, Jimmy."

He flashed her a smile. "You lock, Cassie." He meant to say rock.

"It's my pleasure, Jimmy. So, will you do the deep dive into Jackson's emails for me?"

"Shite yeah!" Jimmy's speech was drifting into lilting Irish profanity. "Anything for you, Cass. Anything," he said.

Cassie hoped he remembered his pledge in the morning.

Chapter 23

SITTING AT HIS desk, Jimmy held his head between his hands, regretting his choice of wine over beer at dinner. Had Jimmy stuck to drinking beer—what he knew and was used to—his head wouldn't throb like a bitch. But no, he had to impress Cassie by showing her he wasn't a simple nerdy man.

Despite Jimmy's impaired mental state, he recalled the promise he made to Cassie. But he had to wait for his head to clear and for the right time to delve through the firm's files. Although it was Saturday morning, there were a handful of staff in the office along with Michelle and stick-your-nose-in-everyone's-business Kayla. Avoiding Kayla's prying eyes when going through Jackson's numerous stored emails was imperative. Nephew or not, Kayla would report him to Michelle if she determined he was breaking the firm's confidentiality rules. Kayla, the loyal soldier.

AT HOME, ON HER PATIO, CASSIE anxiously waited for Jimmy to do the deep dive into Jackson's emails.

Sipping on coffee, Cassie's mind circled like the eye of a tornado. There were far-reaching consequences to uncovering the truth. What if her search led her to discover Jackson, not Bob, was her father? What then? If she was Jackson's daughter, she was conceived the year he and Michelle married. Cassie could only imagine Michelle's reaction. Michelle would come harder at Olivia and her, and Cassie couldn't blame her. Were Cassie in her shoes, she would do the same.

Cassie couldn't imagine her mother being interested in someone like Jackson, let alone sleeping with him. Cassie's mind went where it shouldn't, and she straightened in her chair when the thought came to her. It had to be why Jackson was paying Marilyn the money. It was hush money for an unwanted daughter.

Cassie wrapped her arms around her body. Jackson had forced himself on Marilyn. She was the product of rape was the thought that filled Cassie's head.

Marilyn alluded to nothing of the sort, but how did you tell your child she was the product of rape and unwanted by her father?

Oreo's bark shook Cassie out of her reverie. She watched him run up to her with a stick in his mouth. His tail wagging eagerly, he dropped the stick at her feet.

"Thank you, Oreo. That's a very nice stick." Tippy tapping, Oreo looked up with a wide doggie grin. Barking, Oreo ran to the patio's edge and back to Cassie. "But it's not a present for me. Is it? You want me to toss it? Well, there you go." Cassie tossed the stick, and Oreo chased after it.

The air was warming as the Saturday morning wore on, and the sun reached its apex in a stunning blue sky. The outdoors smelled like a sweet summer day.

The patio door opened, and Cassie looked up to see Olivia and George step through and walk to her. "How was the Farmer's market?"

"Never again." George jumped in to answer. He wore tan chinos, a breathable crew neck T-shirt, and loafers. "I told Olivia it would be packed, wall-to-wall people gabbing. And guess what? It was. I wanted quiet on my only day off, and guess what? I didn't get it by going to that market."

Oreo ran toward them with the stick in his mouth and dropped it at George's feet. George picked it up and tossed it fifty yards away.

"Don't be so melodramatic, George." Olivia wore a white poplin skirt and tank top and tied her hair into a braid that fell to the side.

"I'm going upstairs to change into my running gear. I need to go for a run to clear my far-from-relaxed mind." George called Oreo to join him, and he was happy to do so.

"He has a flair for the drama sometimes." Olivia seated herself on the chair beside Cassie. "No matter what George says, I got a great apple pie, a freshly made baguette, amazing cheeses, and cold cuts. I thought of making a bruschetta and charcuterie plate for dinner and apple pie a la mode for dessert."

"Sounds great. Since when did George start running?"

"It's more speed walking. I'm unsure why he suddenly got the itch to damage his knees. I think middle age is sinking in. "He wanted me to join him. As if I have a desire for pain at my age." Olivia leaned back in her chair and turned her face toward the sun to let it pour over her face, and for a while, they sat in silence.

"He looks like a mean runner in his gear," Cassie said when George ran past them in a bright green shirt, shorts, and pristine white running shoes.

"Better to look good than feel good." And he looked great. Olivia followed George with smiling eyes until he disappeared in the distance. "Will Marco be joining us for dinner?"

Cassie nodded. "He texted me earlier and told me he would like to join us."

"He's welcome to Italian night. Dinner's at seven." Olivia felt the hot sun on her face burn hot.

"I already told him he's welcome to dinner, but I'll text him the time."

As quiet as Cassie's voice had been, Olivia heard much more. "Is everything okay, Cassie?"

"Yeah. Yeah. Yeah, everything's fine."

Three yeahs told Olivia it wasn't, but didn't press once she heard George's voice telling her Cassie would only shut down if she did. "You and Marco have seen much of each other lately. Going beyond your scheduled meet-ups." Olivia's pleasant tone gave Cassie the impression of a woman feigning ignorance and nosing around.

"Yeah, about that, I'm sorry. I got … creative."

"I don't know what you're talking about," Olivia said, and Cassie quirked her brow in response. "Okay, I'll admit I know what you were up to. In fairness, I have thirty years of life's experiences on you and whatever you do, I've been there and done it."

"And you have George's supersonic hearing to boot." Taken aback by Cassie's comment, Olivia stared at her. "George confessed to Marco that he eavesdropped on our conversation and told you everything."

"The man is too honest for his good," Olivia muttered. "But you and Marco have been spending a lot of time together." The last word was stretched for emphasis.

"Yeah, we have." Cassie's face unconsciously brightened, and her lips curved into a smile.

"And?"

Cassie wiped the smile off his face when she became conscious of it. "And it's a work in progress."

From somewhere in the depths of the property, Oreo loudly barked, and George could be heard telling him to ignore the squirrel and follow him.

"It seems to me it's gone beyond a work in progress," Olivia said.

There was a brief pause on Cassie's part. "Yeah, it has."

"That's wonderful, Cassie. You should have happiness in your life. But…." Olivia hesitated for a moment. Rolling her eyes to the sky, she said, "Are you using protection?"

Straight to the point, Olivia didn't allude to the topic or lead with small talk. It caught Cassie off guard, and her cheeks flamed. "Jesus. We're not having this conversation, Olivia."

"Yes, young lady, we are."

"I'm not a child, Olivia."

Olivia sensed the rigidity flowing around Cassie, and she said, "I'm sorry. I know you're a grown woman, but you're like a daughter to me, and I want the best for you. Marco's a great young man. He would never hurt you, but accidents happen, and I don't want that for you. You're young and have so much going for you, so much to do, triumphs to realize."

Cassie's anger was replaced with understanding, and she smiled faintly. "I know. We are using protection. He's a doctor, for God's sake."

Olivia saw so much naiveté in the green eyes levelled at her. "Honey, he's a man with active hormones that, once triggered by a beautiful woman, takes over common sense and the ability to differentiate right from wrong." Olivia held a hand up to silence Cassie when she opened her mouth to speak. "I like Marco a lot, and I know he cares for you, but you're discovering emotions and urges that are a natural part of life but are new to you, and you need to learn how to navigate through them." Olivia let Cassie digest that for a moment. "I want you to be proud of your decisions as a woman. I want you to make your mother proud of the woman she raised."

A spurt of unreasonable anger flared through Cassie, and she stated flatly, "Why? My mother was a liar. All she did was lie to me."

Olivia stared at Cassie dumbfounded. "What's that supposed to mean? What makes you say something like that, Cassie?"

Without saying a word, Cassie stood up abruptly and stormed from the patio into the house.

Chapter 24

STANDING BY KAYLA'S desk, Cassie watched Michelle walk toward her office. Michelle was class and elegance in the white slim-fitting zip-back dress and red pointed heels. Her blond hair was twisted into a French bun, and her humourless green eyes, shaded behind dark lenses, looked straight ahead. She held a brown Valextra briefcase in her left hand, and its matching handbag hung from her right elbow.

As Michelle crossed the floor toward her office, the staff, like Moses and the Red Sea, cleared a path for the she-devil incarnate to walk through.

"I'm sorry to keep you waiting, Sandy," Michelle said, ignoring Kayla. "Please come in. Lunch set up, Kayla?"

"It is, Michelle. I got the garden salad and quiche you ordered, and the same for Sandy. I can heat it in the microwave if it's cold." Kayla started to follow Michelle into her office, but Michelle held a hand up to stop her and closed the door in her jowly face. "Have a seat, Sandy."

Cassie sat at the table. "If you're running behind, we can do this later."

Michelle dropped her handbag and briefcase on her desk and, reaching for the stack of messages, flipped through them. "I was in court all morning and am starving. I haven't eaten since last night," she said, setting the pink slips on the desk and moving to scan her emails. There were too many to address in a few minutes, and she minimized the laptop screen. "I had Kayla get you apple juice, but if you prefer coffee, help yourself."

"Apple juice is good." Cassie popped the lid on the bottle and drank as if to prove her point.

Michelle sat on the opposite side of the table. Her right arm draped on the back of the chair, she crossed her legs and fixed probing eyes on Cassie, studying her.

Cassie's pin-straight hair fell around her face to her shoulders. She wore a thin gold necklace around her neck and cubic zirconia studs at her ears. Michelle could spot diamond simulants from any angle. Cassie wore baby-blue skinny ankle pants and a tan shirt. All off the rack, with no designer labels or a showy appearance, Cassie looked the picture of innocence. For a girl her age with her available means, Cassie lacked the vanity beauty like hers triggered.

It was a mystery to Michelle what drew Jackson's eye to Cassie. Jackson liked his interns vain and adventurous.

"I wanted to follow up on our last conversation to see if we as a firm are fulfilling our duty in providing our interns with the right insights into the legal profession." Michelle signalled Cassie to help herself to the food before her.

Sour waves of nausea rose in Cassie. Her stomach pitched, rolled, and threatened to expel her breakfast bagel. How did she speak to Michelle's comment straight-faced? Cassie had no interest in anything legal when she came to work at the firm and less now that she had seen what she had. The lying, cheating, and doing what you must to win the case at all costs made law an acquired taste.

Cassie thought quickly of something to say.

"I'm still undecided, but I'm enjoying learning all aspects of the business. Jackson has allowed me to do various administrative tasks, which is good for me. I believe you need to start from the bottom and work your way up to get a good grasp of what you do here." Cassie kept her expression neutral and hoped Michelle didn't read into the lie.

Michelle drew her brows together, and Cassie's breath hitched when she feared she was caught in the lie. "That's a refreshing and prudent approach," Michelle said, to Cassie's relief. "You haven't touched your quiche. If you don't like it, I can have Kayla get something else."

Surprised she passed Michelle's scrutiny, most of the sickness in her stomach passed, and Cassie forked a mouthful of quiche. "This is excellent."

"It is. Kayla gets it from my favourite restaurant." Michelle dug into her salad. "So, tell me, Sandy, aside from filling out Jackson's expense reports, what else does he have you doing?"

"I manage his schedule, luncheon appointments, schedule his court cases, do research," Cassie added the last part to cover for the time she spent in the filing room.

"That seems like something Mimi, his assistant, should handle." Michelle poured Perrier into her glass and set the empty bottle on the table.

"Jackson said Mimi is overworked. I don't mind doing it." Cassie topped her fork with quiche.

Michelle took a long sip of her Perrier water as she studied Cassie's face. An overworked Mimi wasn't a thing. Unlike Michelle, who handled dozens of high-profile cases yearly, Jackson clocked in four or five—at most. Not enough to keep his sizable staff occupied. Jackson, the Wisenheimer who wasn't. Michelle wondered what Mimi did for Jackson to fall in his favour for him to get the assistant an assistant. Michelle made a mental note to tell Kayla to keep a vigilant eye on Mimi.

"Still, Mimi's paid a good salary to perform a function and should," Michelle said as agreeably as she could.

Cassie panicked. Cassie didn't mean for her fib to get Mimi in trouble. "I don't mind, Michelle. I really don't. I…." Cassie hesitated as she considered the idea of telling Michelle everything.

"And you what, Sandy? Just say what's on your mind." Michelle levelled her eyes at Cassie, who looked on the verge of telling her everything.

Cassie rose and walked to the window to avoid Michelle's piercing gaze. Cassie could see the compellingly blue sky and felt the mercilessly hot sun beat down on her through the windowpane. The traffic noise from below was muted but discernible: beeping horns and revving engines. Cassie watched blue herons winging their way across the sky on their way to dive for their meal in the waters of Lake Ontario.

What woman welcomed the news her husband might have fathered a child early in their marriage, Cassie thought. How would Michelle react knowing that the child was sifting through his laptop and manipulating the firm's personnel to give her confidential information?

Common sense prevailed, and Cassie said, "I wanted to tell you that Jackson gave me access to his case files and stuff. Not that I needlessly go through them, but it's been bothering me since I heard you don't like the interns getting open access. I don't want to be accused of getting into confidential information." Cassie lied with a straight face. She was becoming fluent in lying.

"I see." Michelle masked her disappointment.

"I meant to tell Jackson about my uneasiness, but I didn't want to risk losing my internship. I'm sorry." Cassie fibbed with such confidence Michelle wasn't able to discern fact from fiction.

Michelle said, "I'm sorry you've been distressed over it. Jackson should have had our human resources department vet you. Had they done so, they would have had you sign an NDA, a non-disclosure agreement, when you started to work for us. I can draft a copy for you to sign."

Cassie could only stare at Michelle. There was no outburst or condemnation, only understanding and reasonableness. Michelle wasn't the wicked woman Olivia had painted, Cassie concluded.

Cassie said, "Thank you. That would alleviate my concerns and help me seamlessly perform my duties."

Michelle nodded. "It would, and thank you for being open and honest, Sandy. In the spirit of honesty, I would appreciate our discussions, no matter how frivolous, remain between us."

"Yes, of course, Michelle."

Part III

The End

The most human thing you can do is to love and forgive

—M.L. Lexi

Chapter 25

OLIVIA HAD EVERY light turned on, and the bedroom was blindingly bright as she paced. George watched her from the bed, his eyes volleying back and forth like a tennis ball.

"What could she mean by saying Marilyn was a liar?" Olivia's wine-red silk robe flowed behind her like a superhero's cape. "Do you think she knows?"

"I don't know, Livy. Why don't you ask her?" George sipped at his Cabernet.

George's hair was damp from his shower, and he wore his HOT FOR YOU underpants, which he realized wouldn't get him anywhere tonight. Not in the mood Olivia was in. Olivia was too agitated, and it would take hours to calm herself when she got like this.

"I did. Cassie got up and walked away and locked herself in her room." Restless, Olivia paced faster. "She's been in her room since then. I took her the charcuterie plate, but she wouldn't open the door."

"She knew that was only a ruse to get into her bedroom and talk to her."

Olivia stopped and turned to face George. "Am I that predictable?"

"I'd say more calculating. Oreo and Marco with her?"

Nodding, Olivia ran a frustrated hand through her loose hair. "She lets them into her bedroom."

"Sit with me." George patted the empty mattress beside him. "Have your glass of wine. It'll calm you."

Olivia dismissed him with a wave of her hand. "This has to do with whatever she's been involved in the past few weeks. I wanted to ask her that too, but…."

"She walked away." George finished, stretched his legs out on the bed, and crossed them at the ankles.

Olivia frowned worriedly. "What if Cassie's found out the truth, George? What if Cassie knows?"

George confidently shook his head. "She doesn't."

Olivia's brow winged. "You say that with confidence."

"If she had already uncovered the truth, she would have blamed you for not telling her. Drink. It'll calm you down." George handed Olivia the glass of wine when she fell back onto the edge of the bed. "You need to consider coming clean and telling Cassie everything, Livy. Meaning no holding back any details. If Cassie is digging into things, she will find out sooner or later and hate you for not telling her."

Olivia took a sizeable, numbing gulp of wine. "I can't, George. I just can't."

"Unfortunately, you will have to do it. I would talk to Cassie, but it has to come from you. Bob told you all his secrets before his death and asked you to do it."

Olivia sipped again, more deeply this time.

Chapter 26

THE LATE NIGHT promised to be clear, and the weight of the summer heat hung in the air. Once Cassie thought Olivia and George had fallen asleep, she went to the pool for a swim. She needed to swim away the anxiety in her.

Marco accompanied her because he couldn't pass up looking at her in the leopard print bikini.

The lampposts cast cones of light around the pool. The blue pool water rippled with every stroke of Cassie's arms. From the pool's edge, forbidden to bark so as to not wake Olivia and George, Oreo quietly tippy-tapped as he followed Cassie. Marco sat at a lounge chair and watched Cassie, appreciating the beauty of her curves in the tiny bikini.

After twenty laps, Cassie swam to the pool's edge and raised herself out of the water. "You should jump in for a swim." Cassie took the towel Marco handed her. "The water's great."

Marco wore jeans, a plaid shirt, and, at his sockless feet, loafers. He had his legs stretched out, crossed at the ankles. "I'm good watching you. Besides, I don't have a bathing suit." He picked up a tired Oreo and set him on his lap. A couple of head scratches sent Oreo into a deep sleep.

"You could go without. It's not as if Oreo and I haven't seen you naked before." Cassie nudged Marco's leg over so she could sit on the edge of the chaise.

"Olivia hasn't, and if she's watching us from her bedroom window…."

"Which she is. I thought she was asleep, but there she is, by the window, watching us. She's a nosy bitch." Cassie angrily jumped in to say.

"Yes. Well. Anyway, if Olivia sees me in all my glory, she may get the notion to dump George for me," Marco jokingly said but didn't get a laugh or even a smirk from Cassie. Cassie's thoughts were elsewhere, and Marco knew where. "Be patient, Cass. Jimmy told you he needed time to go through the system without attracting attention from his team or anyone at the firm."

Cassie wrapped her wet hair with the towel after she dried herself. "I know he's taking his time to avoid getting noticed or leave a paper trail. I feel guilty about deceiving Auntie Michelle. I've lied to her, making things up while she's been supportive and accommodating." Cassie threw on her polo shirt and shorts over her damp bikini. "The more I get to know her, the more I see that she's not as bad as Olivia made her out to be. Auntie Michelle is tough, but I would be too if I had the pressure she carries on her shoulders of running a multi-million dollar company with hundreds of employees. You know?"

"I do." Marco gently ran a hand over Oreo's fur as he snored. "But…."

"No. No buts. Olivia is out of line for saying all the nasty things she did about Auntie Michelle." Cassie slipped her hands into her shorts pockets in defiance.

Marco merely lifted a brow. "I'm on your side, Cass. Always." He took her hand and pulled her beside him, and Cassie stretched out close to him on the lounge chair. "All I'm saying is they've known one another longer than you have, and sometimes familiarity gives you a better insight into things."

Cassie looked into Marco's eyes. "Olivia knew Auntie Michelle at a very dark time in her life, and maybe she saw things through that darkness."

Marco slid an arm around Cassie's shoulder, and she snuggled into him. "That may be so, but age is like a wisdom metre. The older you get, the more experiences touch your life and shape your rationale, and become the foundation for judging the people and happenings in your life."

"That theory only works that way for some. Some people only see through tunnel vision."

In the distance, the howl of a wolf sounded, and its mate replied with her distinctive whine.

"It works out the same for everyone. The difference is that our rudimentary core experiences are different. Some of us might have fewer core experiences due to the simpler or the privileged life we lead while others have had a more difficult life and have been subjected to more obstacles."

Cassie understood Marco's underlying meaning was about her. "That's a lot to digest this late in the night." She snuggled close to Marco and breathed in the smell of sweat and his cologne. Sexy, she thought.

"It is. I'm sorry." Marco slipped into a moment of silence. "Cassie, what if you find out you're the reason for your mother accepting the payments and that Jackson is your father? I mean, what then?"

Cassie's grief and disappointment overcame her as they had in the past few days, and she said nothing for fear of Marco hearing it in her voice. But Cassie didn't have to say anything for Marco to feel the tension in her body.

Marco hugged Cassie tighter. "No matter the outcome, Cass, I'll be here for you for as long as you let me," Marco said, and the sober tone of his voice told her he meant it.

"What if I'm... you know. What will you think of me then?"

Marco looked into her misted green eyes. "It makes no difference to me, Cass. Throughout our lives, we reinvent ourselves many times over. Whether through a new career, a life-changing event, or even a new outfit or haircut, we change ourselves, and you will, too—if it comes to that. But you shouldn't have to. You're a loving, caring, respectful, smart woman. No matter where you come from or who your parents are, you're perfect the way you are."

The words struck her heart and etched themselves there. Here was love, Cassie thought, her heart swelling large. Cassie covered his mouth with hers. "You always know the right thing to say."

"Because what I say comes from here." Marco took her hand and rested it on his heart. "And because I love you absolutely and completely, without reservation, Cass."

Cassie tilted her eyes up to his. "And my money has nothing to do with how you feel about me."

The comment made his eyebrows lift. "You're about to become broke and homeless." Marco kissed her. His breath was warm, and his lips moist. "Regardless of that fact, I still love you unconditionally."

It wasn't the first time Marco had told Cassie he loved her, but it was the first time Cassie said, "I love you too, Marco."

The words filled his heart with the love from her he'd wanted for so long. He gathered her in and clung tightly as if not wanting to let go. They remained that way into the night.

Chapter 27

THE TEXT PING on Cassie's cell phone woke her. Cassie rolled over and fumbled for her phone on the night table, careful not to wake Marco beside her in bed. Looking at the screen, Cassie saw Jimmy's text. The single smiley face emoji told Cassie Jimmy had deposited what he found from his sweep into the draft folder of their shared email account.

Cassie sat up in bed with an abrupt jolt, waking Marco. "I'm too tired, Cass. I have to get some sleep. I'm due at the hospital," he opened one eye to scan the clock radio on the night table, "in two hours."

"No, babe, I'm not looking for an early morning delight. I'm sorry to wake you. Go back to sleep," she told Marco, and he did.

Reaching for her iPad on the night table, Cassie opened the shared email account and reviewed the data dump Jimmy uploaded. Cassie expected two dozen emails, but Jesus! Cassie saw over five hundred, a heap more than she expected.

The house was asleep. In the deafening silence, Cassie flipped from email to email and went paler and paler. Jackson's fraudulence went beyond what Cassie imagined or asked Jimmy to find.

"Christ! All I asked Jimmy to do was to filter emails by the words 'transfer money,'" Cassie murmured, flipping through the emails. "I never imagined I'd see.... Holy shit!" Cassie stopped muttering when she opened the email authorizing the transfer of three thousand dollars to account number 907137311187.

Cassie blinked, eyes wide in shock as she reached deep into her mental file. The last five digits, 11187, matched the number sequence of her mother's bank account.

Cassie took a deep breath before opening the email sent on the thirteenth of the month from Jackson's account. There was another authorized three thousand dollars transfer to the same 11187 account.

At that moment, Cassie's world lurched into a darkness that changed her entire existence. Cassie's heart thudded like a jackhammer in her chest. She turned to nudge Marco out of sleep but stopped herself. Marco looked peaceful, deep in sleep, and Cassie couldn't bring herself to wake him.

But Cassie was wide awake, and her heart thumped. Cassie pushed off the bed. Her feet were silent on the wood floor, and still, Oreo stirred in his bed by the window. Oreo opened one eye and looked at Cassie.

Cassie raised her finger to her lips to silence Oreo before he let out a bark. "Stay, Oreo. Go back to sleep," she said, fumbling her way through the darkened room and picking up her polo shirt and shorts off the floor, where they landed when Marco tossed them over his shoulder after undressing her.

Tiptoeing out of the bedroom, Cassie went to the kitchen, filled a glass with tap water, and tossed it back to calm herself. Cassie's breathing slowed and controlled, and she walked out to the patio. Her head, however, was still clouded, and she decided to go for a walk on the estate grounds to clear it.

It was five a.m., and the sounds of dawn filled the stillness: chirping birds, quacking ducks, and the resident woodpecker hammered on the tree bark. The rising sun lit the sky pink and purple. The cooler morning temperature that came before the burning sun heated the day was comfortable.

Cassie walked across the manicured lawn through the brush and followed the carved path to the creek. She sat by the stream at the nurse log draped in green moss. The chirping of birds coming from somewhere above was crisp and loud. In the steady trickling water of the creek amid its tinkling sound, the bullfrogs that took summer residence there croaked their song.

There was always a lot of energy and enthusiasm in the early morning, but Cassie heard none of the pleasant sounds around her as she shook her head in disbelief. Jackson, the man who wooed her to his bed, was her father. Cassie tried to shake the sick feeling the thought stirred in her.

"Jesus H. Christ! How messed up is that?"

Cassie's attempt to swallow the vile taste rising in her throat failed, and she threw up. Wiping her mouth with the back of her hand, Cassie sank deep in thought.

How could Jackson not know she was his daughter? Cassie had never met her father and didn't know him, but didn't parents instinctively know their children? Wasn't a father supposed to recognize the woman who carried his DNA?

Cassie was more confused than ever when she asked why Bob Huntley took her in when she appeared on his doorstep saying she was his daughter. He had to have known she wasn't his daughter, yet he took her in.

She looked pitiful, pale, and thin as a rake. Maybe Bob took pity on her.

"No. No, that couldn't be it," Cassie reasoned, remembering the birth certificate inked with Bob Huntley's name as her father.

Above her, a large flock of Canada geese soaring across the sky honked in V formation.

Cassie's unanswered questions remained unanswered. Why was Bob's name on the birth certificate? Why was Jackson paying her mother the money? Jimmy told her about the circulating rumours Jackson paid hush money to silence women for his indiscretions. If Jackson's money paid to silence her mother, why did he find the need to make an appearance at the nursing home to talk to her?

Cassie thought back to that time and pictured the moment in her head. Her mother knew Jackson, and he knew her.

Cassie buried her face in her hands. She should have left things alone as Olivia asked her to. Cassie should have never pursued a relationship with Michelle that never existed or would come to pass.

In the pit of Cassie's stomach, a knot tightened.

Did Cassie tell Michelle who her husband was and what he did? She would want to be told if Marco cheated on her and treated women like his personal play toys.

The truth could be so ugly and painful that it can upend your life, but without it, your reason for being is futile. Cassie remembered Marco telling her.

Nibbles crossed to the creek, took a sip of water, and climbed onto the log. Wrinkling his nose, Nibbles stared at Cassie.

"Oreo's not with me, Nibbles," she said, looking up at the squirrel with sad eyes. Cassie heard Oreo bark then before he walked up to the log and stared at his archrival with eyes narrowed to thin slits. "Where did you come from?"

"He helped me track you." Marco appeared from around the Linden tree. He had slipped into the jeans and plaid shirt he wore last night. His hair was windblown, and a day's beard growth shadowed his jaw. "I saw the files on your cell phone." He held his hands up in the air, palms out. "I didn't mean to go through your phone. I got worried when I woke up and didn't find you in bed beside me. Your phone was lying there."

Cassie looked down at her kneaded hands. "I guess you saw everything."

Marco nodded. "Enough. Are you all right, Cass?"

Tossing up her head, she said, "I'm not." There were tears in Cassie's eyes, and Marco wrapped her in his arms. She pressed her face on the hard plane of his chest and cried.

Chapter 28

OLIVIA SMELLED THE freshness of the land and heard the soothing sound of trickling water from the creek as she walked around the Linden tree. The morning sun shone through the thick canopy of green leaves on treetops and dappled the ground like a knitted doily. Far above, in the blue sky, birds flew, landed on tree branches, and chipped in song.

At Oreo's bark, Cassie looked up and aimed moist green eyes at Olivia. "Marco can't keep his mouth shut."

Olivia scratched Oreo's head when he raced forward with his tongue lolling. She wore faded jeans and a lavender shirt. "He's worried about you, and now, looking at your state, I am too." Olivia sat at the log beside Cassie while Oreo set off to lap water from the brook.

Cassie's hair was rumpled, and her eyes were red-rimmed from crying. "You would be, too, if you saw what I did." The green eyes studied Olivia, a frank and cagey stare for a moment. "Did Marco tell you everything?" Cassie asked to ensure she didn't reveal more than necessary.

Olivia shrugged. "Marco gave me the Reader's Digest version. He was in a rush to get to the hospital. Why don't you tell me your version of the story?"

Cassie Looked up to the sky where an eagle soared, wings spread wide. If only she could fly away and be as free as that bird, Cassie would get away from everyone and everything, she thought. Cassie wouldn't have to deal with the confusion, anger, shame, and feeling the world was against her.

"Cassie, I want to help you, but I can't without knowing the whole story. You can talk to me."

Cassie's hotly annoyed green eyes narrowed. "I can't, Olivia. You were against me reaching out to Auntie Michele from the onset." Olivia merely lifted a brow, a sign Cassie should modulate her attitude. "Sorry, but you did want to keep me away from her."

Olivia gave Cassie a steadfast look. "Not because I wanted to keep you apart, but because I didn't want you to get hurt."

By the brook's edge, Oreo raised one eye, then the other at the bullfrog straddling the rock croaking at him.

Cassie let out a long, defeated sigh. "Yeah, well, it's too late for that."

Cassie's face was darkly tanned, and hundreds of golden freckles were scattered over her cheeks and nose. She looked like a little girl needing hugs and affection, but the pain in Cassie's eyes told Olivia this wasn't such a simple fix.

"Why don't you tell me everything, Cassie? Start from the beginning."

With hesitation, Cassie told Olivia her story from the beginning. As Cassie did, the pain in her eyes intensified. "It's unethical and immoral, Olivia. It's sick." Cassie rose to pace. "It hurts to know I was discarded for money Mom willingly accepted. It hurts because I thought Daddy was my father, but he, too, lied."

"I'm sorry, Cassie." Olivia's heart broke, observing the hurt and broken expression on Cassie's face. "Bob loved you, Cassie. That's undeniable."

Bored with the frog, who did nothing but croak and stare with listless eyes, Oreo walked away and disappeared into the brush.

"I don't know that anymore." Cassie covered her face with her hands. "My heart hurts. I'm angry for being lied to by the people I've loved."

Watching the pain engulf Cassie, Olivia felt her stomach jump to her throat. For all of Olivia's efforts to keep this moment from materializing, here it was, and the truth she had kept from Cassie had to be told. Olivia closed her eyes for a moment before she rose. Walking to Cassie, Olivia wrapped her arms around her. "I need to tell you something, Cassie, but not here. Michelle must be present when I do."

Punchy with anger, Cassie pulled away from Olivia's embrace. "What does she have to do with anything?" Cassie's hotly annoyed green eyes narrowed. "Tell me. Now, Olivia,"

Olivia shook her head. "You and Michelle both need to hear this."

Chapter 29

IT WAS A long, interminable drive to Huntley Knut & Associates. In the passenger seat, Cassie sat quietly, besieged by a storm of conflicting emotions surging through her while Olivia's stomach turned and churned the entire time. Now in Michelle's office, Cassie sat on the sofa, staring at her hands resting on her thighs, and Michelle beside her had her venomous stare peeled on Olivia, whose stomach did somersaults.

Both women would be gravely affected by what Olivia had to say. Michelle wasn't as much a concern to Olivia as Cassie was. Michelle was a big girl with many life experiences in her pocket, and as much as she looked the other way when it came to Jackson's frolicking, she knew what he was. Cassie was young, vulnerable, and naïve to how people hurt people for no reason other than selfishness. There would be more hurt when Olivia told her what she knew. The probability of Cassie carrying the pain inside her for years, gnawing at her, eating her up inside was high.

Olivia hoped Cassie would find purpose rather than grow angry and become cynical and bitter because the truth had to be told. It was time.

Olivia walked to the glass-plated wall and closed the blinds to prevent the staff's prying eyes from looking into Michelle's office and giving them the necessary privacy.

"Say what you have to, Olivia. I have work to do," Michelle said in an imposing tone.

There wasn't a good way to deliver the news, and under Cassie's unblinking stare, Olivia point-blank said, "Jackson is not your father, Cassie."

"Of course, he's not," Michelle jumped in to say, her tone indignant. "Why would you make such a ludicrous comment, Olivia?" Michelle stared at Olivia, eyes blazing. "Oh, I see. Is that what Bob told you? If he did, he was shooting his mouth off to serve his purpose—as usual."

Olivia's eyes locked on Michelle's. "Bob said no such thing."

"Then why make such a preposterous statement?" Michelle propelled herself from the sofa and stormed to the sideboard to pour a tall vodka drink. Every conversation with Olivia led to drinking.

Olivia sat on the chair by the sofa. "Because it's what Cassie believes after the information she dug up on him."

"It's Sandy. She knows me as Sandy Olsson," Cassie said from between clenched teeth.

"Michelle knows who you are. She's known all along. Isn't that right, Michelle?" Olivia remarked with confidence.

"Of course, I knew who you were." Michelle exchanged a long, hard look with Cassie.

It was an option Cassie had never considered, and the surprise was apparent on her face. "You knew who I was the entire time."

"I did. Of course I did," Michelle spoke coolly, but her eyes were ripe and hot.

Cassie's body went limp at the admission. "So, the lunches you set up with me were a ruse for what?"

"To figure out what you were doing." Olivia put in before Michelle could inject her alternative facts. "Isn't that right, Michelle? Did you have someone follow Cassie and report back to you her movements?"

"I had my secretary report on Cassie's activities," Michelle admitted, but only after Olivia's persuading, piercing gaze fixed on her.

Cassie took a steadying breath and turned to study the woman whose blood she believed ran through her veins. Michelle knew who she was, and instead of getting to know her and bringing her into the fold of her family circle, she had her followed and spied on like a criminal. The hurt and disappointment was huge.

Cassie let out a long, disheartened sigh. "You knew who I was, and still, you had me followed?"

"It's what she does. It's who Michelle is. Her interests above everyone else's, no matter who she hurts along the way," Olivia said, her voice rising, hardening. "Isn't that right, Michelle?"

"I need to know everything transpiring in my company to protect my interests," Michelle asserted impatiently.

"I'm family." Cassie's eyes were slits when she hissed the words.

Sitting on the sofa, Michelle draped her arms across its back and crossed her long legs. "You're nothing to me."

Cassie looked at Michelle. She wore a red, tapered pantsuit with matching pointed pumps. The chain at her neck was an intricate, thick gold weave, posh and expensive. Her makeup was perfect, as was the honey-blonde hair that flowed in perfect, shiny waves around her face. It differed starkly from the basic white shirt, jeans, and patent flats Cassie and Olivia wore. Yet, amongst the three, Michelle was the one who looked common, cold, and heartless. Or so Cassie thought.

Cassie now understood Olivia's disdain and dislike for Michelle. Now, Cassie understood that Bob's reason for distancing himself from Michelle was to protect her and not out of selfishness or control.

"Ignore her, Cassie. This has nothing to do with the bullshit she's trying to pass as a business practice and everything to do with her thinking you were becoming Jackson's play toy for the summer. Isn't that right, Michelle?" Olivia held firm eyes on Michelle.

Cassie gazed at Michelle in amazement. "Are you telling me your actions are derived from jealousy?" Cassie snapped.

"Not entirely, but that was a part of it," Olivia confirmed.

"Well, I can assure you, I had no interest whatsoever in an old lech with an ego the size of Pluto. Not that he didn't try, by the way. The man is a walking erection." Cassie exploded irately, simultaneously wincing in disgust. "Ew, really?"

As much as the comment drove a hot spear of anger into Michelle, she remained poised. Giving Cassie and Olivia the satisfaction of a reaction would make Michelle look fragile. She wasn't fragile.

Michelle swallowed a mouthful of vodka. "It's nothing of the sort. It's as I said. I need to keep track of what goes on in my company, and I will not allow anything to get past me," Michelle said, swimming in feigned confidence.

Above her green eyes, Olivia's brows shot up. "I'd refill your glass with vodka and prepare for what Cassie and I have to say."

"What could she possibly have to say of interest," Michelle abruptly said and then turned to Olivia. "And I sure as hell have no interest in anything you say."

"For once in your life, Michelle, shut up and listen. Two ears, one mouth," Olivia said. Not accustomed to being spoken that way, Michelle's mouth hung open, and she remained quiet. Olivia looked over at Cassie, whose eyes were shadowed with exhaustion. It hurt Olivia's heart to see. "Cassie, honey, tell Michelle what you uncovered."

"I can't," Cassie murmured.

"She uncovered nothing because she had access to nothing. I run a tight ship." Michelle took a long swallow of her drink.

"You tell yourself that." Olivia's tone was sarcastic with patronizing undertones. "Aside from being smarter and more level-headed than some grown-ups, kids today are more computer-savvy than we'll ever be. They will access, hack, or whatever the term is, into any system if they set their minds."

A frown line deepened momentarily between Michelle's eyebrows. "What are you saying?"

"That Cassie inherited the Huntley resourceful gene and easily accessed the files you guard so tightly," Olivia assured Cassie she wouldn't implicate Jimmy as her accomplice, and she didn't.

Michelle closed her mouth, lips pressed together in a straight, thin line. "Who gave you access? I demand you tell me now?"

"Really? That's what interests you most," Cassie snapped.

Michelle gave Cassie a quick, angry glance. "This is my business, and my focus is staying on top of things.

Now, tell me who gave you access." Ice dripped from Michelle's words.

Hugging a protective arm around Cassie's shoulders, Olivia said, "Cassie, put everything out of your mind and tell Michelle what she wants to know. It's the only way to shut her up."

Cassie warred with her mind to snap clear. When it had, Cassie took a deep breath and said, "It was simple to access Jackson's laptop. You, old people, should rethink your simplistic passwords." Cassie flashed a cynical smile and proceeded to tell Michelle everything she uncovered. "The last money transfer was as recent as a few weeks ago."

Olivia saw Michelle's expression transform from defiance into one of genuine surprise. "You didn't know about the money transfers."

When Michelle started to speak, she couldn't formulate the words to answer Olivia. Instead, Michelle rose and walked to the window to give them her back. A move she used in the courtroom when she needed to collect herself. Michelle stood at the window, not moving, not saying anything.

Below, the waterfront was thronged with people enjoying the summer day. On the boardwalk, mothers pushed strollers, children played or ran through the water spray in the water park, couples leisurely strolled, and bicyclists weaved to avoid them. In the lake, kayakers and sailboats glided on smooth, blue water. A family of Geese majestically waddled their way about the park, taking no notice of anyone in their way.

Michelle's back to Olivia and Cassie, she said, "I knew about the money transfers, but not that Jackson continued to request the funds."

On busy Front Street, traffic pushed off when the light turned green.

"What do you mean, Michelle?" Olivia asked.

"I caught the money transfers a few years back and insisted Jackson immediately stop. Jackson promised he would." Michelle's voice was subdued.

"Did he tell you the reason for the transfers?" Olivia took Michelle's silence as a yes. "And still, you told him to stop them." Olivia waited for a response. None came.

Olivia looked at Cassie. There was no turning back now. Even if it meant propelling Cassie into a world of hurt she'd carry for years, gnawing at her insides, Olivia had to tell all. Cassie had to know the truth.

"That was probably when you saw Jackson speak to your mother. He was there to tell her she would no longer receive the monthly payments, which was maintenance for you, Cassie. And it wasn't three thousand dollars you should have received monthly, but ninety-nine hundred," Olivia said.

Cassie was so shocked by what she heard she became momentarily speechless for a moment. "Christ! The man who seduced me is my father and pocketed sixty-nine hundred dollars meant for me," she said when she found her voice.

Michelle turned to Cassie with a look that could have turned her into stone. "Don't lie. Your mother has received ninety-nine hundred dollars for years."

"No, she didn't. The deposits to my mother's account have been three thousand dollars. I can prove it," Cassie said defiantly.

The understanding washed over Michelle all at once. Jackson had pocketed the difference all these years. Michelle's jaw clenched as anger began to war with fury.

"And you demanded he cut us off. We needed that money to survive. My mom was barely keeping us above water even with her working at the nursing home." Cassie's tone was steel. "You didn't even need the money. The entitlement of the rich is sickening."

"Please calm down, Cassie," Olivia said when she saw the pain in her eyes and heard the hurt in her tone.

"How can I calm down when I find out that my father was short-changing us money we desperately needed to survive." More tears wanted to come, but Cassie's anger didn't permit them to flow.

"Yes, you stopped receiving the money because of Michelle's actions, and Jackson pocketed money meant for you, but as I said, honey, Jackson's not your father," Olivia said.

Chapter 30

CASSIE'S HEAD SWIMMING, she pressed her finger to her tearful eyes. "Who is my father?"

As let down and disillusioned as Cassie felt, she had to know everything. Olivia pressed on. "Robert Huntley … Senior is your father. That's Michelle and Bob's father." Olivia watched Michelle standing by the window, tightly wrapping her arms around her body.

Cassie stared at Olivia openmouthed with confusion in her eyes. "What are you saying?"

There wasn't a good way to deliver the news, and Olivia jumped right into it. "Robert had an affair with your mother while she worked at the Huntley Estate as a housemaid."

Cassie gave Olivia a hard eye. "He was married. Mom would never do anything like that."

"He was in his fifties, and your mother was … young. Very young. She was impressionable, easily manipulated," Olivia said. "Two years into the affair…."

"Jesus! It went on for two years?" Cassie buried her face in her hands as the letdown in the woman she looked up to hit strong. The woman who impressed on her that self-respect, dignity, and honour made the person was an adulterer and she the outcome. The humiliation on top of the hurt was more than Cassie could stand. "Has everyone lied my entire life?" She gasped against the pain biting down on her.

Olivia picked up a tissue from the box on the coffee table and handed it to Cassie. "I don't think your mom purposely lied to you, Cassie. Sometimes people make mistakes and say what they believe they should to protect or shield us from the pain or...."

"You tell yourself that," Cassie cut off Olivia mid-sentence.

"I will tell you everything that Bob told me before his death if you let me, Cassie."

Cassie's heart sank deep in her chest. "Daddy knew all of this and never told me. He lied to me, too. But then, of course, he would. He wasn't my father."

Olivia nodded and admitted, "Yes, Bob knew you weren't his daughter. He knew all along because Bob had a vasectomy when he and I were married, so he wouldn't give me the child I wanted."

Michelle's lips slanted into a sneer. "That's the prince that was my brother."

Olivia let the comment pass. "But then, you knew also, didn't you, Michelle?" An unpleasant silence fell in the room and hung like a dark cloud. "Michelle told Bob as much when she visited him to demand he sign over everything their mother left him to her," Olivia said after some time.

Wide-eyed, Cassie stared at Olivia. "She came to your house, and you didn't say?"

"It was one of the times we were out, and by the time we came home, she was gone. Bob didn't say anything to me until much later when he told me Michelle had come equipped with the paperwork for him to sign that would deed the house and turn over the money their mother left him to her. He refused. Bob told Michelle the house and money were willed to you. He said you were the one who took care of him and put up with his mood swings and idiosyncrasies, which got worse when he got sick. He loved you, Cassie." Olivia closed her hand over Cassie's. "Michelle, however, told him you didn't deserve it because you were the product of an affair their father had with your mother. Isn't that right, Michelle?" Olivia's eyes held Michelle's intently.

Michelle didn't react. She stood by the sideboard, pouring her third vodka.

Olivia pushed on. "Bob told me you came across Katherine's diaries, that's Michelle and Bob's mother when you were cleaning up her bedroom for you to occupy."

The comment jogged Cassie's memory. "Yeah, that's right. I found six books in shoe boxes stashed in the back of the closet. I gave them to him. I didn't know they were diaries."

"Well, they were diaries, Katherine's diaries. Whether as an escape or looking to publish her memoirs, we'll never know. Whatever the reason, Katherine documented her and Robert's life in those diaries. And there was a lot to read." Olivia turned to Michelle. "Pay attention, Michelle, because what Bob told me will be news to you too."

"Bob didn't tell me about finding Mom's diaries, and I doubt anything he told you would interest me." Michelle's eyes were calm, yet her voice was barely controlled.

"I believe it will interest you. So, sit down, Michelle, and listen up." Olivia levelled a green gaze at Michelle to indicate she was serious. Reluctantly, Michelle sat in the chair Olivia vacated. "Two years into the affair, Marilyn told Robert she was pregnant. Robert pressed her to have an abortion, but Marilyn vehemently refused. She told him she would never get rid of the baby she already loved more than anything." Olivia squeezed Cassie's hand. "Those were Marilyn's exact words, honey."

"More like she saw a cash cow," Michelle murmured.

Olivia observed cynical, distrustful Michelle and felt sympathy for her. Her disposition was the consequence of her profession and partly due to the lack of love from the man she gave so much to. "You know, Michelle, some of us believe money is not the end all."

"Money is everything to everyone." Michelle's words were larded with innuendo.

Olivia slowly shook her head with sadness. "Jackson overheard the conversation between Robert and Marilyn. Jackson proposed to Robert a way out of the situation by offering to dispose of Marilyn in exchange for marriage to Michelle."

Michelle's face was drained of colour. "That's a blatant lie. Daddy would never pawn me like cheap wares."

Olivia's eyebrows lifted in mild disdain. "Both you and I know your father would readily sacrifice his flesh and blood, anyone, to benefit his interest. It's a trait you inherited, Michelle." Olivia dropped her eyes to Michelle, who was still reeling from being bartered for a favour. "Robert talked Michelle into marrying Jackson, and in return, Jackson removed Marilyn from the picture. Tit for tat."

"Bob came up with this nonsense in a moment of delusion. He had become delusional toward the end of his life. The tumour was doing crazy things to his mind. I spoke to him. I know." Michelle sent vodka streaming down her throat.

"Bob may have been dying from a brain tumour and was forgetful, but when he spoke to me, his faculties were intact. It was the case when he spoke to you. His faculties were so intact he refused to sign your document," Olivia said.

"For Christ's sake, Olivia. Why are you defending Bob after what he did to you?" Michelle's tone was an impatient hiss.

Arguing seemed futile, and Olivia didn't dignify Michelle's comment with a response. "Although you found proof that Jackson was the one who made the monthly transfers to your mother's account, Cassie, the request didn't come from him or Robert. Robert wasn't a generous man. You know that's a fact, Michelle. Your father was as stingy with his money as he was at expressing his love."

"Don't speak about Daddy in that manner. You haven't earned the right." The fury simmered in Michelle's words.

Olivia dismissed Michelle and turned to Cassie. "The money was sent to your mother at Katherine's request. Katherine felt sorry for Marilyn, a broke young woman with a child on the way cast out into the cold to fend for herself. According to her diary, Katherine told Jackson to set up the monthly transfer to Marilyn. Katherine asked Jackson to make it happen without involving her or mentioning her name, or she would tell Michelle about his deal with Robert." Olivia went silent for a moment to let Michelle process that.

"From the generous salary Katherine drew from the firm, she directed a monthly payment of ninety-nine hundred dollars, an amount that would keep it from government or the firm's scrutiny, to be paid to Jackson as a monthly retainer. Jackson agreed to handle the transfers, keep Marilyn's name out of the transaction, and keep Robert from finding out."

The look of total bafflement on Michelle's face for being used by her mother, father, and husband was hard to miss. At the same time, Cassie's brow furrowed as she worked the thread through her head.

"Let me get this straight," Cassie jumped in to say when she had thought things through. "You're telling me that my biological father had nothing to do with supporting my mother after getting rid of her and me. That my half-sister cut off that support, and to top that, Jackson, for years, pocketed the money made available through the generosity of the cockled woman."

Olivia nodded. "That's the sum of it."

The sound of introspection hung heavy in the room.

"Christ! You people are so dysfunctional I regret wanting to be associated with the Huntly name. My mother and I struggled financially. I was fatherless, homeless, at the mercy of strangers for my survival, but we had more dignity in our pinky than you imperious Huntleys combined." Under Cassie's unblinking stare, Michelle tried not to squirm. "You were so right to try to keep me away from this family, Olivia."

"I'm sorry, Cassie. I'm sorry I didn't tell you any of this sooner. I'm sorry…."

"You have nothing to apologize for, Olivia. It's me who owes you an apology for doubting you." Cassie's eyes cut away from Olivia to Michelle. "To think I could build a relationship with people I considered family now seems ludicrous and the furthest thing from my mind. You're as cold and heartless as your father, our father, and as Daddy, or our brother, my half-brother, said you were." The tears started down Cassie's face, and Olivia held her while she cried her shock, with Michelle silently staring at some distant point.

"I will tell you what I told Bob." Olivia brushed the loose tendrils of hair from Cassie's face. "As much as

Michelle had choices and she could have chosen the righteous path, don't blame her. She wasn't given the love and support from those she trusted most. She didn't get the love she wanted from her father, whom she looked up to, admired, and adored. She hasn't gotten it from the husband she loves. As for Katherine, she was intimidated and broken by your father, Michelle. Robert was a hard, demanding man. I'm sure she would have protected you instead of blackmailing Jackson if she could. Maybe financially supporting Marilyn was her way to redeem herself."

"Don't speak for her or me. You don't know us." Michelle retorted, but the words came out very thin.

"Maybe not, but one thing I do know is that you deserve love, to be taken care of by the man who loves you unconditionally. And that man is out there," Olive said.

For a long moment, the office was infinitely silent. The hum of the air conditioner and Michelle's breathing were the only sounds in the room.

"I need to tell you one last thing, Michelle. I say it not to hurt you but to open your eyes to who Jackson is. Jackson not only asked for your hand in marriage, but he asked Robert to make him a partner and add his name to the firm's marquee. Your father initially refused, but Jackson blackmailed him by threatening to tell you everything. There is no honour amongst narcissists. Your father agreed to the partnership with the stipulation Jackson's name only be added to the marquee on his death."

Shock widened Michelle's eyes instantly before she straightened up in her seat. Digging deep inside her for dignity, she tried to formulate the words to defend Jackson but came up empty.

"Luckily for you, after his first major heart attack, facing his mortality, in a desperate attempt at salvation, Robert confessed to your mother about the affair, the baby he produced, his deal with Jackson, everything."

Michelle raised an eyebrow and crossed her arms. "So what? You claim she knew all that."

"Yes, she did, but along with the confession, Robert gave Katherine the combination to the safe in his office. Where she found vital documents."

"What vital documents?"

"Your father wrote a new will that gave your mother fifty percent of the firm and twenty-five to you and Bob."

Michelle sucked in a breath. "That's bullshit. Daddy left me fifty percent of the firm."

"That's what your mother led you to believe. Bob was his son, after all, Michelle."

"No, he wasn't. Daddy disowned Bob long ago."

Change would come for Michelle when she had more time to digest and disentangle the emotions of betrayal, disillusionment and hurt stirring in her. Not today, Oliva thought. "As I said, death has a way of reaching into your soul and opening your eyes to see the mistakes you've made during your lifetime. It triggers the need for repentance. Robert wasn't the emotional, apologetic type, so giving Bob a quarter of the firm was his way to make amends to his son."

Michelle's blinding pain of betrayal consumed her, and she reacted angrily. "He may have been his son, but I'm the one who did everything he wanted. I stayed behind. I did everything right, the Huntley way."

"You did, Michelle, but I wasn't finished." Olivia walked to the sideboard and brought back two bottles of water. One bottle was for Cassie, who dabbed her watery eyes with a tissue. The other bottle was for Michelle, who would have preferred another shot of vodka, but she accepted it and drank deeply. "Bob told your mother he didn't want his share of the firm. He signed it over to you because he believed you deserved it."

"I don't believe it."

"It's the truth. In exchange…."

"There we go. Tit for tat was Bob's way."

"What he asked for in return was for your mother to leave the house to him. Bob wanted more than anything to return to his childhood home."

"You're lying." Michelle's body deflated like an airless balloon.

Olivia reached into her handbag and handed Michelle a diary embossed with the words *For Michelle* on the face of it. "It's all right there. Katherine was quite the author. It's her way to make amends for failing you, for not protecting you from your father when you most needed it. There's a lot of interesting reading. This is another document Katherine found in the safe. It's from your father." Olivia turned over the thick document. "You may need it if you decide you're worthy of love and the partner you truly deserve."

"What is it?" Michelle's voice was a whisper.

"It's the document your father had Jackson sign that stipulates that when his name is added on the firm's marquee, he relinquishes his right to proprietorship or share of the firm. It also specifies Jackson has no right to ownership of anything you own. I think it's a prenup of sorts. It ensures Jackson doesn't get his hands on the firm or what belongs to your sons and you."

Michelle was mid-sip and choked out a little bit of water. "Jackson would never sign such a document."

Olivia's mouth twitched. "See how thick that document is. My guess is your father knew Jackson was a lousy solicitor, and his weakness was his ego, and he played on that. Jackson was so keen on getting his name on the marquee next to the Huntley name that he signed the Non-Disparagement agreement your father put together without reading it. And Jackson really should have." Olivia's brows lifted to drive the point.

Michelle could see her father doing just that. As much as it filled Michelle with genuine regret that Robert had debased Jackson to the lowest form of legal trickery, she felt a sense of relief.

"It's all in the diary. Make time to read it, Michelle."

Michelle snatched the book from Olivia's hand. "You've read it all."

"Bob asked me to. His memory was limited toward the end of his life. He couldn't remember everything but recalled enough to tell me I'd find all the answers in the diaries I needed to protect Cassie. He loved Cassie and wanted her to get what she deserved." Olivia looked at Michelle with eyes that had seen everything. "You have the tools, Michelle. You can change your story anytime."

Olivia gathered Cassie off the sofa and left Michelle with her private thoughts.

Epilogue

LOVE IS NOT something you find. It finds you when you least expect it. Family worked along the same lines—or so Cassie believed. The people who fortuitously came into Cassie's life, Olivia, George, Sondra, Malcolm, and Marco, were her family. That went for Oreo, too.

Michelle might be a blood relative, but months later, she hadn't reached out to Cassie to build the familial relationship she had hoped for. In the deep recesses of Cassie's mind, she hoped Michelle would reach out once she put behind her divorce to Jackson, which she asked for after the meeting in her office.

Hope, the eternal spring.

Deny, deny, and more denial was Jackson's response to Michelle's accusations. When Michelle handed him the divorce papers to sign, Jackson panicked. Sensing his cushy lifestyle imploding, Jackson threatened to take half of everything she possessed.

Jackson's threats evaporated when Michelle produced the contract he signed for Robert and the data Cassie mined in the firm's system. "That document is null and void," Jackson pushed the document across the desk at Michelle. "I didn't know about those clauses."

"Christ, Jackson, I've always known you were a third-rate solicitor at best, but even you can't be that stupid. That contract is as valid today as it was when you signed it years ago," Michelle said.

They sat across from each other in Michelle's office, her desk providing the necessary barrier between them she needed.

Filtering the anger surging in him out of his voice and replacing it with the sweet tone that always got him what he wanted, Jackson said, "But baby...."

Michelle cut him off. "Your terms of endearment aren't going to work anymore, Jackson."

Nervous and anxious at the impending collapse of his affluent lifestyle, Jackson rose to pace her office. "Think of the boys. They need their father, a male figure in their life."

With her eyes rolled slightly upward, Michelle said, "And I will get them a male figure to look up to. One who is not a womanizer. A man who will teach them respect for women is not duplicitous, and they can rely on him to be there for them."

Jackson stopped pacing and aimed blazing eyes at Michelle. "What the fuck does that mean? I'm their father."

"You are, and they're grown men. They can decide for themselves if they want you in their life or not. I will support their decision either way. As for me, I'm nothing more than the woman you've been cheating on all of our married life and using to line your pockets. And I'm done, Jackson. I want you out of my life and gone from my house by the time I get home tonight."

"It's my home, too," Jackson snapped.

Michelle waved the document in the air as a reminder. "This says otherwise." Feeling empowered and in control of her destiny, Michelle now spoke in a mild tone. "Your name will come off the marquee tonight. Your electronic devices are being cleared from your office by Jimmy as we speak. I've changed the passwords to my bank account and all company accounts. I want you to clear out your office. You have twenty minutes to clear your things and go. I want no vestige of you here or in my life."

In their years of marriage, no matter what Jackson did, Michelle never spoke with the determination he saw in her eyes at that moment. "How am I supposed to survive?" Jackson snapped, tossing the contents of his glass back.

Michelle surveyed Jackson with a glance that took in every detail of the man she fell in love with and endured all these years. He was dressed to the nines in a gray silk suit, a baby blue shirt, and a matching tie bought with her money and befitting his inflated ego. A pair of five hundred dollar Bvlgari sunglasses was nestled in the dyed blonde hair. Midlife crisis was hitting hard. His eyes were glassy and empty, and Michelle wondered what she had seen in him all these years. Love was blind.

"You have the millions of dollars you stole from Mom and me over the years." Michelle laughed and shook her head. "You've spent every dime on your whores. Pretence does come at a high price," Michelle said, watching defeat washing over Jackson all at once.

Michelle buzzed Kayla to send in the security guards standing by outside to escort Jackson to his office and off the firm's premises. Karma was a wonderful, vindictive bitch, Michelle thought. Cassie thought the same when Jimmy, between mouthfuls of the hamburger Malcolm handed him, recounted the story circulating in the offices of Huntley and Associates.

"I'm telling you as I heard it. Michelle had security watch over him as he packed his office to make sure he didn't take company property. Then they escorted him out of the office empty handed. Turned out everything in the office belonged to Michelle." Jimmy licked off the ketchup that dripped on his yellow polo shirt when he bit into his hamburger.

"It's ketchup, Jimmy, that'll come off when you wash it." Cassie made a rolling hand gesture to speed him along.

"Michelle had me deactivate Jackson's entry card, cancel his cell phone service, and take all his electronic devices. She had me shut down his email and change all the internal passwords to deny his access. I told you Michelle could be one scary bitch when you cross her, but I'm glad she's finally rid of that loser," Jimmy said, leaving Cassie staring into the distance, lost in her thoughts. "Malcolm, my man, I'll take a hot dog if you have one going."

"Jimmy, if you don't mind, there are others, as in Olivia, George, Marco, Malcolm, Cassie, Nicola, and Oreo, who'd like to eat." Sondra shot Jimmy a look that made him wither like a cornered animal.

"She's right, Jimmy. You've been stuffing your face since we got here." Nicola's big, dark eyes shot lasers at Jimmy.

Nicola had olive skin, short, dark hair, straight-cut bangs above big eyes slathered with dark makeup, and her lips with black gloss. Her nails were manicured black, and on her thumbs, she wore a gold-plated ring. She wore a black T-shirt, shorts, and combat ankle boots. She was Jimmy's kindred soul.

"I can't say I understand this vibe you have going, but I like you, girl." Sondra fist-bumped Nicola.

"Like clucking chickens, they're scary when they flock together," Jimmy muttered.

"I heard that," Sondra and Nicola jointly said.

"Peace out, Sondra. Jimmy is Cassie's guest and a buddy. There's more than enough to go around." Malcolm tilted his chin at Marco, signalling to go into the house and get a pack of hot dogs, stat.

"He could be Christ walking on goddamn water. I couldn't care less. I'm starving. What about you?" Sondra asked Nicola, who nodded emphatically. "Serve Nicola, me, and Oreo before, buddy here gets anything else. Understood." Sondra commanded, and Oreo plopped on his butt by the barbecue. "And, for your information, never tell a starving woman to peace out if you treasure the family jewels."

Nicola flashed Sondra a smile. "I don't get this white sundress and sandals vibe you have going, but I like you, girl."

"Beer anyone." George offered to sidetrack the conversation.

Malcolm picked up on the coded message George SOSd to a distressed brother and jumped at the offer. "I'll take one."

"I'm not done with you," Sondra said.

"Woman, you're doing my head in," Malcolm added the hot dogs Marco brought him on the grill.

"I think the boy will need something stronger than beer, George. This argument could go on for another fifteen minutes. That's how long it will take for the hot dogs to cook." Olivia sat back on the lounge chair and sipped on her strawberry margarita.

"You're not wrong about that." George poured three fingers of Johnny Walker over ice into a tumbler and brought it to Malcolm. "Gulp it down. Doctor's orders. It'll calm your nerves," George murmured.

Sondra's brows winged. "I heard that."

"He didn't say anything." Malcolm erected his protective field around George. The brotherhood was strong.

"The booze has you growing a testicle, Malcolm?" Sondra replied with a steady, unblinking gaze.

Quietly, Marco walked backwards and away from the situation. He was a lover, not a fighter.

"Are they always like that?" Jimmy asked Cassie, watching Malcolm and Sondra bicker.

"Most days," Cassie said with a crystalline understanding that this whacky collection of people was her family and wouldn't have it any other way. Cassie only wished Michelle and her nephews could share in the moment. Patience was a virtue. "Finish telling me about Michelle."

Jimmy turned his eyes away from the Shakespearean tragedy before him to Cassie. "Michelle sent a memo to the staff, clients, banks, and anyone on her email list advising of Jackson's dissolution of employment. That's what she called it, 'dissolution of employment.' Get the double entendre? Hysterical." Jimmy laughed and took a pull of his beer. "Exactly what that asshole deserves."

"It is." Cassie sat back in her chair and looked over to Marco.

Marco looked like the helpless puppy who wanted to rescue his friend from the attacking Pitbull. An intelligent man, Marco knew that coming to Malcolm's defence when Sondra yapped on with spirit wouldn't work well for him or his friend. With a great capacity for remaining silent when necessary, Marco took a long pull of his beer and said a silent prayer for Malcolm.

Marco was loyal and caring. He would never be the man Jackson Knut or Robert James Huntley Senior were

Marco was the man who saw the world the way Cassie did and wanted the things she wanted. The best part was that he loved her and would never hurt her.

Cassie's life was complete.

You *can* change your story anytime. Cassie had.

Sneak peek at M.L. Lexi's new novel

THE DECEITFUL WOMAN

One

Five Years Later

THE AIR WAS ripe with the scent of coffee and the sound of grinding beans. A commercial for a dream Caribbean destination flashed from the television screen that hung between the menu boards. Despacito flowed from the overhead speakers. Those waiting to place their order bobbed their heads to its picante rhythm. The tables and the bench seats were crowded with the after-school crowd of voluble teenagers in hoodies, jeans, and white trainers ingesting more caffeine than needed.

Lacy leaned a hip against the counter and stared at her daughter. "Organic milk only, Maddie," Lacy said and watched Madison on the opposite side of the counter set down the carton of skim milk in her hand and reach into the refrigerator for the organic milk.

Madison waved the carton of milk at her mother. "Satisfied?" she said after pouring into the tall coffee cup.

Nodding, Lacy flicked her eyes to the cold-cut sandwich in the display case. "And how about one of those subs, heated, to go?

"It's a Panino, not a sub." Madison snapped the lid on the coffee cup and placed it on the counter before Lacy.

"It's a sub. That Panino crap is snobbish gobbledygook to triple the price." Lacy took a sip from her cup and hummed. "Christ, that's a good cup of coffee."

"You know none of this is free. It's deducted from my pay." Madison reached for the tong, clamped it on the Panino Lacy signalled, and walked it to the hot press. "You complain enough as it is about my meagre paycheque, and if you continue to eat it away, I'm never bringing home that executive salary you want."

Blue eyes steady on defiant blue eyes, Lacy looked at the face so much like hers. Madison's waist-long glossy black hair was pulled back into a ponytail, accentuating her heart-shaped face, with large, round eyes crowned with long, dark lashes. Madison's face had the silky smoothness of a twenty-two-year-old, which Lacy, at seventeen years her senior, had lost to lines etched by a hard life.

Madison was lean with a fit frame, a genetic trait Lacy or possibly her father had handed down—if she knew who he was. Madison was five-eight, four inches taller than her mother. She wore her customary jeans, a white T-shirt, and scuffed running shoes from many years of use.

Lacy sighed. "Oh, honey, I stopped expecting anything of any consequence from you long ago."

Madison set the bagged Panino on the counter. "Well, ditto, Mother dearest."

Lacy's smile spread wide at Madison's sharp tongue, which came from her side of the family. "Touché daughter, touché."

Despacito segued into Paris by The Chainsmokers. Some in the crowd mouthed the words to the song, and Lacy's eyebrows furrowed. Music died a gruesome death after the eighties.

"Raisin cinnamon bagel, toasted with butter, Madison," Mike called out from the cash register.

Madison acknowledged the order with a "Coming up."

Wiping her hands dry on the front of the green apron emblazoned with the words *The Coffee Shop*, Madison slid on a pair of disposable gloves. Reaching for the bagel, she cut it in half with the serrated knife and set it to toast.

"What's that?" Madison asked when Lacy set the papers on the counter.

"Those are copies of the monthly bills. You're going to start contributing to the household expenses, Maddie. I've carried you for long enough."

Madison sucked in air and hissed it out. Her mother could be such a depressant injector. "Can we have this conversation later, Mother? As you can see, I'm swamped right now." She put the bagel with two containers of butter, a plastic knife, and a napkin into a paper bag and handed it to the girl in the green and burgundy plaid uniform scrolling through her cell phone. The girl didn't acknowledge or thank Madison. That was the sum of her life.

"Whether we talk about it now or later, the outcome is the same. You're an adult now and need to pay your way, and you're contributing to the household expenses." Lacy reached into her tote, and Madison assumed her mother was going for her cigarettes.

"I told you, you can't smoke in here? You think as a nurse you'd know better." Madison hooked the tongs onto a blueberry muffin and bagged it. Pointing at table five, she signalled to pick up the bag.

"I was reaching for the additional bills, internet, taxes, and miscellaneous to add to the pile."

"Madison, two Grande coffees, a scone with peanut butter, and a strawberry cake lollipop." Mike handed the young pimpled face kid change from a ten-dollar bill. "All separate orders."

Madison reached for two cups and flipped the handle on the urn to let the coffee pour. "You know I make a pittance and can barely make ends meet. How am I supposed to contribute to pay the bills?"

Lacy watched her daughter manage the multiple orders with ease. If only Madison would put her skills to better use. "You'll have to figure it out. It's about time you carried your weight. We're splitting costs fifty-fifty."

Madison slammed the two coffee cups on the counter. "I can't afford that, and you make way more money than I do at this crappy job." She wouldn't dare tell her mother that much of her pay cheque went toward paying for the private investigator working for her for the past seven months. That wasn't a conversation she was ready or willing to spar over with her mother.

"Madison, this," Mike raised a hand, palm out and circled it before Madison, "is not the attitude we want to convey to our customers. There's too much negativity there."

Madison turned and flashed Mike a forced all teeth smile. "Better?"

Mike's slash of dark eyebrows rose. "Right. Well, I need three regulars. Leave room for cream."

"Go away, Mother. You're funking up my workspace and generating too much negativity in peaceful Madison."

Lacy rolled her eyes dramatically and reached for the bag containing the Panino. "This is my dinner, so make arrangements for yours," she said as Amber Fox-Roche flashed on the television screen.

The words to her lauded, syndicated show Tell Me All appeared on the screen before fading, and the camera closed in on her. Amber's straight, black hair was perfectly groomed, and her makeup was expertly applied. Her large, cerulean eyes were dusted in bronze, her high cheekbones rouged, and her full lips traced in dark plum lipstick. Her nails were long, painted salmon-pink on manicured hands.

Amber wore diamond studs at her ears, a gold chain around her long neck, gold bangle bracelets on her wrist, and a gold wedding band encrusted with diamonds. The sharp red suit she wore with matching stilettos suited her tall, slim frame and added to the poised, confident image she portrayed on camera. On the matching gray chair beside Amber, handsome Keanu Reeves up-talked the newly released John Wick movie. Amber smiled with all her warmth and force.

The epitome of manufactured perfection, Lacy thought, staring at Amber. As beautiful as Amber was on the outside, she was morally corrupt on the inside. Or was the term moral turpitude more apt? The public would know who the real Amber Fox-Roche was if Madison told all.

Lacy flicked her eyes from the television toward her daughter, who had stopped what she was doing and transfixed her eyes on Amber. The look on Madison's face was a worrisome cagey stare out of blue eyes.

Nothing good came from that look.

Coming Soon

The Complete Woman
The Conflicted Woman
The Spiteful Woman
The Tortured Woman

The Relentless Woman Duology

The Relentless Woman
The Vindictive Women

The Unbreakable Woman Trilogy

The Unbreakable Woman
The Brave Woman
The Valiant Woman

Contact us

Email us at mllexiauthor@gmail.com to receive emails whenever M.L. Lexi publishes a new book. There is no charge or obligation and your information will remain confidential.

Visit us at www.mllexi.com to read excerpts of upcoming releases.